MW01131435

End in Sight

The Chronicles of Kerrigan, Volume 6

W.J. May

Published by Dark Shadow Publishing, 2015.

The Chronicles of Kerrigan

End in Sight

Book VI

By

Also by W.J. May

Blood Red Series
Courage Runs Red
The Night Watch

Daughters of Darkness: Victoria's Journey
Huntress
Coveted (A Vampire & Paranormal Romance)
Victoria

Hidden Secrets Saga
Seventh Mark - Part 1
Seventh Mark - Part 2
Marked By Destiny
Compelled
Fate's Intervention

The Chronicles of Kerrigan
Rae of Hope
Dark Nebula
House of Cards
Royal Tea
Under Fire
End in Sight

The Hidden Secrets Saga
Seventh Mark (part 1 & 2)

The Senseless Series
Radium Halos
Radium Halos - Part 2

Nonsense

Standalone
Shadow of Doubt (Part 1 & 2)
Five Shades of Fantasy
Glow - A Young Adult Fantasy Sampler
Shadow of Doubt - Part 1
Shadow of Doubt - Part 2
Four and a Half Shades of Fantasy
Full Moon
Dream Fighter
What Creeps in the Night
Forest of the Forbidden
HuNted
Arcane Forest: A Fantasy Anthology
Ancient Blood of the Vampire and Werewolf

W.J. May

The Chronicles of Kerrigan

Book I - *Rae of Hope* is FREE!
 Book Trailer:
 http://www.youtube.com/watch?v=gILAwXxx8MU
 Book II - *Dark Nebula*
 Book Trailer:
 http://www.youtube.com/watch?v=Ca24STi_bFM
 Book III - *House of Cards*
 Book IV - *Royal Tea*
 Book V - *Under Fire*
 Book VI - *End in Sight*
 Book VII – *Hidden Darkness* – COMING JANUARY 2016
 Book VIII – *Twisted Together*
 ** *Turn to the end of END IN SIGHT for sneak peaks at the new covers and information on Hidden Darkness & Twisted Together.*

Coming Christmas 2015!!

A Novella of the Chronicles of Kerrigan.
A prequel on how Simon Kerrigan met Beth!!

Coming this Christmas

Sometimes the heart sees
what is invisible to the eye.

Novella Prequel
Chronicles of Kerrigan

Check out W.J. May's Facebook Page or subscribe to her Newsletter for more details!!

Find W.J. May

Website:
http://www.wanitamay.yolasite.com
Facebook:
https://www.facebook.com/pages/Author-WJ-May-FAN-PAGE/141170442608149
Newsletter:
SIGN UP FOR W.J. May's Newsletter to find out about new releases, updates, cover reveals and even freebies!
http://eepurl.com/97aYf

Description:

END IN SIGHT is the 6th Book of W.J. May's bestselling series, The Chronicles of Kerrigan.

When life couldn't get any more confusing, fate steps in and throws a curveball.

Rae Kerrigan should be ecstatic. She's found her mother and Devon has admitted he wants nothing more than to be with her. Except Jennifer, her mentor, was someone she thought she could trust and it turns out she was after Rae for the same reason as Lanford had tried her first year at Guilder.

There is a new face for the enemy now. Jonathon Cromfield. Except he's not really new, is he?

Rae must go charging head first into danger in order to protect the ones she loves and like her father, no one is going to stand in her way.

End in Sight is the sixth book in the Chronicles of Kerrigan series. Book 1, *Rae of Hope* is currently FREE.

Follow Rae Kerrigan as she learns about the tattoo on her back that gives her supernatural powers, as she learns of her father's evil intentions and as she tries to figure out how coming of age, falling love and high-packed action fighting isn't as easy as the comic books make it look.

<u>Series Order:</u>
Rae of Hope
Dark Nebula
House of Cards
Royal Tea
Under Fire
End in Sight

... book 7 and 8 titles to be released at the end of End in Sight!

We're born, we live, we die.
It's that simple.
At least, it's supposed to be...

Chapter 1

"It's not Jonathon Cromfield," Carter said flatly, staring at the image. His body stood rigid and tight, exhaustion clearly showing on his face but his eyes were defiant.

Devon, still dressed in jeans and a t-shirt and looking worse for wear himself, leaned forward. "It is, sir," he pointed to the caption scribbled at the bottom of the page, "look."

Carter threw his hands up in exasperation. "No, *that's* Jonathon Cromfield." He gestured to the drawing. "I'm saying, *it's* not Jonathon Cromfield. The man died over five hundred years ago. He's not the mastermind pulling the strings behind what's happening now. It's impossible."

"There's no date of death. At least from what I can remember," Devon continued tentatively, giving Rae the automatic benefit of the doubt no matter how outlandish it seemed. He glanced at her, his blue eyes bright. "It just says he was born in 1491—"

"That proves nothing," Carter insisted, crossing his arms over his chest and looking down at them as if they were children—younger children, that is. "Just that he hadn't yet died when the drawing was commissioned."

Rae squinted as she stared at the picture intently. Same neatly trimmed curls. Same devious look sparkling deep in his eyes. Yes, definitely. It was the same man. She'd seen him just an hour ago, standing in her living room...from twelve years ago. *When did my life get this confusing?!* She nearly laughed out loud. *Just before I turned sixteen, and it just keeps getting more confusing every day.* "It's him," she repeated firmly. "That's the man I saw. I'm one hundred-percent positive."

"It's not poss—"

"James," Beth, Rae's mother, cut Carter off, "it's him."

"Okay, so, it's him." Carter's face paled, but he didn't argue with Beth. "I don't get it. I've seen a lot, but this..." He shook his head. "How does this make sense?"

Rae's face scrunched in consternation. Figures, Carter. Sure, she could swear it up and down all day, but the second her mother opened her mouth, he was an instant believer...

"Not the time, Rae," Devon murmured, guessing her thoughts before she spoke them. She shot him a petulant look, but held her tongue. He chuckled quietly and put his arm over her shoulder.

"Well, what about his tatù?" Beth asked doubtfully.

There was no power that allowed a person to live forever, but perhaps he could have planted himself within certain dreams and memories before death?

Carter shook his head. "His tatù was similar to Julian's—he could predict the future. That's why we have his drawings. It's what made him so valuable to Henry VIII. The king thought Cromfield was his best shot at getting a son. In a way, he's one of the reasons why Guilder was built to begin with."

"Who's Julian?" Beth leaned over and whispered in Rae's ear.

Rae glanced at her quickly. "Oh—right." In the whirlwind of everything that had happened in the last twenty-four hours, Rae had forgotten how confused her poor mother must be, how much she was taking on faith. "Julian's one of us. He's a good friend. He went to school with me, but was in Devon's class—a year older. They both graduated last year and started working for the Privy Council together. He's living on Guilder's campus, helping mentor, like Devon. You'll meet him soon—he's a great friend, one of my best." There was so much she wanted to tell her mom and knew now wasn't the time.

"Which still leaves the question: if Cromfield died half a century ago—how was it that you saw him talking to Jennifer in Beth's memory?" Devon asked with a frown.

"I don't know..." Rae admitted. "But I know one person who could help us find out." She looked up at Carter expectantly.

He held her gaze for a second before lifting his hands. "I already told you, Rae, I have my best agents combing the city for Jennifer, but it's not that simple!"

Beth moved closer to Carter. "How's it not that simple?"

Rae watched her mom, but kept her eyes fixed on Carter. "It's not that simple because...Jennifer's basically our best agent. *Was* the PC's best agent. But that doesn't mean she's impossible to find," she added quickly. "Let me and Devon go back out there tonight. Trust me, we'll find the little—"

"*Language*, Miss Kerrigan!"

A new voice interrupted their conversation, and the four of them turned around to see Devon's father, the Dean of Guilder, pacing towards them through the hushed library.

Dean Wardell? Great, Rae closed her eyes in a pained grimace, *here comes my biggest fan.*

The headmaster's gaze fixed automatically on Devon's arm, still circling Rae's shoulder, and Devon lowered it with a telltale flush. That alone should have been enough to set him off. Or perhaps the fact that Rae was dripping ash and blood all over his pristine library. But tonight, he bypassed both of them as his eyes landed on—

"*Beth Kerrigan?!*" he exclaimed, not bothering to lower his voice. His mouth fell open, and before anyone could explain, he rushed forward and embraced her in a huge hug. "I can't believe it! We all thought you were dead. I don't...know quite what to say."

"Perhaps now is not the time." Carter stepped neatly in between them, his eyes making a pointed sweep of the rest of the curious students.

It seemed a casual enough gesture, but Rae thought that maybe there was something a little more deliberate to his move. Something a little more...possessive?

The headmaster stepped back with a self-conscious flush to match his son's. "Of course! My apologies, I just...can't believe you're here." For one of the first times Rae could recall, he actually flashed her a warm smile. "You must be over the moon."

Over the moon? Really? The man made it his life's mission to keep her and Devon apart, except if it meant rescuing his son. He did not like her. There was no hiding that. To see him attempt sympathy or joy seemed as likely as Cromfield being alive. The man probably hated her mother as much as he did her. Rae smiled tentatively in return, nodding and linking her arm through her mother's. "You've no idea."

Then, in what had to be the worst timing in the world, a glob of bloody plaster fell from Rae's shirt onto the ground between them.

The headmaster's eyes cooled as the corners of his mouth turned down. "Rae Kerrigan." He sighed. "I suppose you'll be resuming classes now that you're suspended from the PC?"

Beth's eyes opened wide. "You got suspended? For what?!"

Rae flashed Dean Wardell a sour look before arranging her features to be the perfect mask of innocence. "If you must know, *Mother*, I was suspended for breaking curfew while trying to find you." She turned to Carter with a superior grin. "But I'm sure that doesn't apply anymore now that you're here. And I actually have to give a security briefing on Monday to the future Queen of England. So, if the PC could just officially reinstate me, I'll be—"

"Not so fast." Carter folded his arms over his chest. "As I'm sure you recall, Miss Kerrigan, there were other...mitigating factors that led to your probation. Factors I'm sure you wouldn't like me to go into detail upon now?"

Rae's eyes flickered to Devon for a fraction of a second, before she dropped her eyes to the ground respectfully. "No, sir."

It was bad enough that Devon's own father had guessed the nature of their forbidden relationship without the freaking

President of the Privy Council knowing as well. Although, to be perfectly honest, Rae wasn't sure if Carter was going to say anything. The depth of the emotions Devon had shown him back at Heath Hall had been enough to make the man almost tear up and cry. Not to mention, Carter was a bit more intricately intertwined with the newly reunited Kerrigan family than he had ever let on. Maybe she and Devon were in the clear...if only for now.

"That's what I thought." But beneath Carter's frown, Rae could have sworn she saw a faint twinkle in his eyes. "And of course, I thought you might want to take some of this time to be with your mother. Not only to reconnect, but also..." His voice trailed off as his eyes darted around the crowded library once more.

But also...to protect her.

Rae's throat tightened at the words he couldn't say. Whether Cromfield being alive was believable or not, Rae knew—without a shadow of a doubt—that he was the man behind the attack on her mother. He had given Jennifer the orders to set the fire that killed her father, and he had specifically instructed that her mother be brainwashed and sent away. In other words, he had single-handedly ensured that Rae would grow up an orphan. If he planned to kill Simon Kerrigan, why hadn't he done the same with her mother? Rae refused to consider the thought more thoroughly. It didn't matter, and yet, Rae had been forced to be an orphan.

Every moment she felt lost or alone... Every night when she'd stay up imagining what it would be like having her mother sing her softly to sleep... Explaining tatùs and what would happen to her... Protecting her from the fear of her father's ability... Cromfield was responsible for every single one.

There was no way she was going to freakin' let him get away with it.

"Sir," she muttered urgently under her breath, "if you could just give me a small team to—"

"Then it's settled," Carter said loudly, deliberately ignoring her. "Dean Wardell, I'm sure you can find Beth some suitable housing in the faculty quarters? And while it hardly needs to be said, I think it's definitely best we keep this under wraps for the time being." He gave Wardell a stare that clearly stated the importance of why.

Devon's father cleared his throat. "Yes, of course. It would be my pleasure."

"And as for you, Miss Kerrigan," Carter turned his eyes again on Rae, "the Dean's right. It's time you stop taking time off for work and return to classes. Final exams are only a few months away. If you don't pass...you don't graduate."

Dean Wardell flashed her a look behind Carter's back, and Rae could tell that would be a situation the headmaster would apparently relish. Or be horrified to have her remain another year. She couldn't quite tell which thought crossed his mind.

She held her ground, but lifted her eyebrows a fraction of an inch. "So, that's the plan?" she asked with a lethal calm. "You're...sending me back to school?"

Carter's lips twitched. "Indeed I am. You're a teenager, Miss Kerrigan, and your mother just came back from the grave. It's time you acted like a teenager. Now—off to bed. We'll meet again in my office in the morning to discuss further plans."

And just like that, the unlikely group suddenly disassembled. Rae blinked in delayed shock as everyone around her silently disbursed. Carter swept back to his office as Dean Wardell led Beth up to the faculty quarters. At first, Devon lingered behind with Rae, but after getting a sharp look from his father, he headed abruptly in the opposite direction—leaving Rae alone in the library.

"Excuse me?"

A tentative voice pulled her back to the present and she jumped around in surprise. Then she lowered her gaze. The girl addressing her couldn't have been more than five feet. She was significantly shorter than Molly, who was already the smallest member of their Guilder group. Her frizzy brown hair hung in little braids down her shoulders, and she was staring at Rae as if it was taking every bit of courage she had just to keep her standing upright.

"Uh, yeah?" Rae recovered herself quickly. "I'm sorry, do I know you?"

The girl extended her hand with a cautious smile. "No—I mean—not yet. I just started going here in the fall. My name's Ellie."

Rae glanced between the girl's face and her hand, before shaking her head with a sigh. "You know who I am, don't you?"

The girl faltered with a frown. "Um...yeah, I think I do. You're Rae Kerrigan, right? I was just coming over to intro—"

"Then you know what I can do?"

The words came out sharper than Rae had intended, but right now, she didn't have time to deal with the little Guilder newbies. Whether this girl was going to obsess over her, or just end up fearing her like the rest—Rae would rather she just figured it out on her own.

Ellie's face grew pale. "They say you...you can mimic other people's abilities with your—"

"Then you shouldn't be offering me your hand, should you?" Rae cut her off curtly. "Listen honey, you need to protect your gift, okay? It's the only one you've got," her eyes flickered darkly towards where Carter had just departed, "and you never know who you can trust these days..."

Without another word, she left the girl standing in the middle of the library and swept out the door. She felt a little stab of guilt as she crossed the lawns and headed back to Aumbry House, but honestly...how much could she be expected to deal with today?

She was in no mood to play 'spectacle' to the green little innocents at Guilder. She had an arsonist to track down, an evil mastermind to find, and she still had to somehow squeeze in the time to get to know her long-lost mother *and* somehow pass the school's notorious finals so she could graduate. Little Ellie would have to get by without her.

By the time she got up to her bedroom at the top floor, she was seriously wishing that over the last few years she'd managed to pick up a tatù that allowed her to self-clean. Try as she did to straighten herself up a little on the way back to school, she was still covered in blood—both her own and Jennifer's. Her clothes had been scorched and torn, and the smell of smoke was so deeply infused into her hair, she wondered if she would ever get it out.

Maybe Molly would let her borrow that amazing conditioner she was always raving about from Switzerland. Sure, cinnamon wasn't Rae's favorite scent, but anything was better than—

"AH!"

A wave of electricity strong enough to down a small elephant shot from Rae's hands and sizzled through the room, hitting the opposite wall with a bang. As the smoke cleared, three heads poked up from the floor behind her bed.

"And that's why I had us wait on the ground," Molly said knowingly. "She startles easily."

Rae looked on in shock as Devon and Julian popped up beside her wearing identical grins. The acrid smell of fried metal filled her nostrils and she whirled around to her desk in fright.

"My computer—"

Molly skipped forward with a smile. "Don't worry, I also grabbed your laptop. If you're wondering, I think that scorched circuitry smell is coming from you..." She picked up a lock of Rae's hair between two fingers and grimaced. "Please tell me that's...paint or something."

"Told you—you always have somebody's blood on you nowadays." Devon grinned and planted a swift kiss on her cheek before pulling away and wiping his mouth discreetly.

Rae couldn't move. Whether it was the surprise of having three of her friends break into her room, or the fact that Devon had just kissed her so openly in public...she was having a hard time.

"What are you..." She turned to the side and casually sniffed her hair. "What're you guys doing here?"

"Devon called us," Julian replied. He was sitting in the middle of her bed like nothing had happened—like she hadn't just lit up the room like an over-charged Taser. "I can't believe you actually found your mom, Rae—that's incredible!"

"That was a good shot too," Molly approved, sitting down beside him. "High voltage."

Devon took over. "They came so you could tell them what the hell's been going on since we found Bethany...but maybe you want to..." He bit his lip and looked down.

"Maybe you want to take a shower first," Molly interjected cheerfully. "You look like Carrie at the prom."

Rae glanced in the mirror and winced at the soot and dried blood covering her entire body. No wonder Dean Wardell didn't want her in the library. And no wonder that girl Ellie had looked so scared before. She shook her head with a sigh. Sometimes it startled her...the things she was getting used to.

"I'll be right back," she mumbled. "Make yourselves at home," she said a little louder as the boys raided her mini-fridge and Molly started automatically going through her closet.

Rae felt no shame in swiping Molly's prized conditioner before hopping into the shower for a rinse. An incriminating trail of black and red streamed towards the drain, but before long, it was replaced with the overwhelming scent of cinnamon. Rae basked in the steam for a moment, taking the time to gather her thoughts. So much had changed in just the last two days, she was having trouble keeping up.

Was it even possible that her mother was sleeping just two buildings away? Was it even possible that Rae was going to wake up in a few short hours and see her again?

She turned off the faucet and towel dried as she considered the possibilities. Maybe instead of Rae getting an apartment, Beth would buy a house and they'd both live together. Or maybe her mother would want to get as far away from London and the Privy Council as possible and insist that they both move back to France.

Rae shuddered at the possibility as she pulled on some designer sweat pants Molly had gotten her for Christmas and a matching camisole. Her hair was silky smooth, and instead of winding it up in a messy knot—as had become her custom—she let the wet curls run loose down her back. Two minutes and one wind tatù later, it was perfectly dry.

She couldn't move to France, she thought as she wandered back down the hall to her room. Her entire life was here. Her school, her job. Her face flushed as she thought of the real reason she didn't want to leave. A certain someone had done a damn good job of making her want to stay.

The same certain someone pulled open the door a second before she reached it and swept her inside, planting a quick kiss on her lips.

Her eyes snapped open and she glanced quickly at Julian and Molly before smacking Devon lightly on the chest. "What the hell do you think you're doing?" she murmured between her teeth.

"Give me a break," he grinned, "do you know how long I've wanted to do that?"

Julian smiled. "And it's not like it's some big secret anymore."

Only Molly grimaced. "Except it's not like that's something I want to see every day." She lifted her fingers up to her forehead.

"I'm going to have to electro-shock therapy the image out of my brain. Devon Wardell kissing someone..."

He laughed and threw a pillow at her as the four of them settled down in various positions around the room. "So, how about it, Rae? You up for a little story time?"

Rae leaned back against her desk and crossed her legs in front of her. "I don't even know where to start. The whole thing's such a blur..." Was her mother safe now? Should she call her? It's not like they had time to exchange cell phone numbers. What... She took a deep breath. Carter would make sure her mother was safe. She needed to let that fear go.

"Why don't you start from right before you and Jennifer fought?" Devon suggested.

Julian's eyes grew wide. "You and Jennifer fought?"

"No," Molly shook her head, "start from when you, Devon, and Carter took an impromptu road trip to France."

"Wait—*what*?!" Julian held up his hands to slow things down. "You're going to have to start a lot further back than that. How about when I dropped you out of the window?"

Rae couldn't help but chuckle. It was as good a place as any...

The entire recounting took the better part of an hour—with many interruptions and loud interjections from her friends. It turned out that while she and Devon had been in the French countryside collecting her mother, both Molly and Julian had some adventures of their own. Molly was the unfortunate one who'd been left at the hospital. So, when the place had flooded with Privy Council agents, it was up to her to sell some sort of wild story in her first ever debriefing. Julian, meanwhile, had taken a sixteen-hour trip to Italy for an agency mission of his own. One which he was being far more secretive about than usual.

"You met a girl, didn't you?" Devon demanded with a grin.

Julian flushed. "What? No!"

"I know that look, man."

"Why? 'Cause you've been wearing it ever since little miss big-thing over there started Guilder?"

"I take offense to that!" Devon countered.

"Enough!" Molly held up her hands for peace. Then she turned to Julian with a conspiratorial wink. "So, who is she?"

He ran his fingers back through his long hair. "I have no idea what you guys are talking about! I also don't think I need to remind you that these missions are *confidential.*"

"We'll find out eventually," Rae teased. "I'm sure I'll pick up some tatù that lets me see down into your very soul."

Molly frowned. "Don't you already have one like that?"

"Oh yeah—Carter's!" Rae brightened and stretched out her hand. "Come here, Julian!"

He backed away so fast it was as if she had thrown a ball of fire at him. "Actually...I better call it a night. I have some early morning training then a debriefing." He was out the door as fast as Devon on a good day. "Night guys!"

The other three cracked up as Molly got to her feet also. "I should turn in too. I can't believe they have us going back to classes the day after tomorrow!"

Rae shook her head wearily. "It's going to suck so bad. G'Night, Molls."

Molly disappeared into the hall but shut the door carefully behind her, leaving Devon and Rae alone in the silence that followed. There was nothing but the suddenly deafening sound of a second-hand clock, and after a minute, Rae glanced at him a little self-consciously and stood up.

"Hey, I'm sorry if I got you in trouble with your dad earlier. I didn't mean to—"

But the next second, her voice was silenced by a kiss.

Devon scooped her off her feet and had her down on the bed before she knew what was happening. His mouth trailed frantic, urgent kisses up and down her neck as his hands scrambled to take off his own shirt and then hers, nearly at the same time. A second later, the tops were on the floor.

"Woah there, cowboy!" Rae pulled away for a second and grinned. "Someone's in a hurry."

He smiled back, stroking a stray curl off her forehead. "I thought they'd never leave."

"Are you sure that this is okay?" She lowered her voice and glanced around the room. "I mean, here at Guilder—"

"Why Miss Kerrigan..." His fingers fiddled with the top of her pants and he flashed her a mischievous grin. "Is someone suddenly worried about breaking school rules? I seem to remember helping you sneak in here not so long ago..."

He was kissing her stomach now, and for a moment, she forgot how to breathe.

"This is Madame Elpis, we're talking about." She smothered a giggle as he bit playfully at her hip bone. "Would *you* like to explain it to her?"

For a split second, he paused. But then he shook his head and lowered it back down to hers with a grin. "Trust me, what I have in mind is well worth detention..."

Chapter 2

There weren't many people who could slip past Madame Elpis at six in the morning, but fortunately, Rae's boyfriend happened to have super supernatural powers. He even slipped out without Rae noticing.

When she opened her eyes, there was still an indent in his pillow. All that rested in the recess was a little origami fox. She picked it up and grinned, wondering how long it must have taken him to craft the little guy. It reminded her of her first year at Guilder. One of the first things she and Devon had unofficially bonded over was his fennec fox tatù. She'd known what it was before he even had to tell her, which, apparently, made her one of the few. Of course before she even had a chance to see it, he'd used it to save her life. Just a chance of luck, sort of. The memory made her laugh. She'd walked out of Aumbry House and she glanced around her room. Shoot! This was the room!

They had been doing renovations to this floor and a two by four or something had come crashing out of one of the upper rooms—this room! Devon had moved faster than a train to get her out of the way. She'd crushed on him even back then, and tried to pretend she wasn't interested.

She twirled the little fox lightly between her fingers. Were their lives always going to be so crazy? Was their romance always going to be fueled by adrenaline instead of lazy weekend kisses and midnight walks on the beach? Or the need to keep things hidden? She was getting tired of living a life of secrets.

A shrill alarm burst through her reverie and she hurried to get dressed in something a bit fancier than usual. She was seeing her mother again today, after all. Despite how normal that should sound, it was quite the special occasion.

In the end, she opted for a silk ivory top—collared, but without sleeves—and simple black dress slacks. As she paired it with teardrop earrings and gazed in the mirror, she thought Molly would be proud. Lately, that was her litmus test for everything 'wardrobe'.

To balance out the extra preparations, Rae switched into Jennifer's tatù so as not to be late to the meeting. She shuddered at the thought of Jennifer's betrayal but pushed it away. The tatù was an ability, not the person.

Halfway across the sweeping Guilder lawns, she suddenly stopped and switched out into Devon's. She couldn't brush the feeling aside. Jennifer's tatù just felt wrong, like it was dirty. Rae's blood heated, she swore to never again use the ability unless it was absolutely necessary.

She made it to Carter's office five minutes early, but everyone else was already there. Her mother flashed her a bright smile as she walked inside.

Devon looked up innocently—greeting her for the first time. "Well, good morning," he said with a carefully controlled smile.

Rae flushed and settled down in her seat without really looking at him. "Morning."

Beth's eyes flickered shrewdly between the two, but she let it go as Carter sat forward at his large desk.

He cleared his throat. "So, I've been going through my notes all night and I came to a simple conclusion." His eyes landed on Rae. "I cannot take this to the Privy Council."

There was a moment of silence before—

"*What!?*"

"Sit down, Miss Kerrigan, and let me explain."

Rae hadn't realized she'd jumped to her feet, and she sank back into her chair slowly, keeping her angry eyes fixed on Carter all the while.

"I simply cannot take this drawing," he held it up, "along with the word of Rae Kerrigan, and tell them that a five hundred-year-old madman has suddenly come back to life to mastermind this grand conspiracy. They'd never believe it. Hell—I don't believe it."

Rae gripped the arms on her chair ready to yell, but Beth cut her off. "Why did you say her name like that?" she asked with a frown. "What in the world do you mean: along with the word of Rae Kerrigan?"

Carter hesitated as Rae and Devon exchanged a quick look. How exactly did they tell her mother that in addition to having a tragic past, she could now look forward to a marked future?

Rae cleared her throat and decided to step up to bat. How did her mom not know? The whole amnesia thing was going to be complicated to deal with at times. "We, Kerrigans, are...how should I say it...not quite so highly regarded in certain circles—"

"We're pariahs," Beth interrupted sharply. "That's what you're trying to say."

"Only by people who don't know you," Devon interjected softly. "Anyone who's spent any amount of time with Rae is quick to see her true colors. That she's the complete antithesis of her father. Rae has proven herself time after time." He turned to Carter. "Which is why her word, along with what she saw in Jennifer's memory, should be enough to launch an investigation."

Carter shook his head. "While I admire your sentiment, it simply doesn't stretch beyond the people in this school. To the rest of the tatù world, a Kerrigan's a Kerrigan. It's bad enough I'm going to have to tell them that not only was Jennifer Jones a rogue agent this entire time, but that we let her get away."

Rae leapt to her feet again, unable to control herself. "And what exactly is the Privy Council doing about that? As much as I despise her, Jennifer's a world-class talent. Every second we waste here is another second she has to completely disappear. You're the president of the Privy Council! We need people on the ground now."

As usual, Carter was unfazed, except for the single eyebrow that rose as she mentioned president. Nobody was supposed to know about that, let alone shout it out at the top of someone's voice. "Miss Kerrigan, I don't know if you're using some sort of new jumping tatù, but I suggest you take a seat so I can continue this meeting." Rae sank sullenly into her chair and he continued, "I can guarantee I want to find Jenn—Miss Jones as much as you do." His eyes flickered to Beth. "I'll make it my personal mission. But like I said, the Privy Council has had people in place since the explosion by the hospital. The entire city is on lock-down, she won't get far."

Devon's hands twitched and he balled them up into impatient fists, clearly as unwilling to sit on the sidelines as Rae was. "With all due respect sir, if you've benched us, why exactly are we here?"

Carter frowned as if it was the most obvious thing in the world. "You're here, Mr. Wardell, because while Jennifer Jones is a threat, Jonathon Cromfield *is* the mastermind behind this entire catastrophe."

"But you just said—"

"I said I can't take this to the Privy Council," Carter repeated. "That doesn't mean that it shouldn't remain our top priority. We're just going to have to keep it...off the books."

Rae shook her head. "Off the books? What does that mean? I can't have any supplies? A team, people to work with?"

Much to her surprise, Carter actually chuckled. "How spoiled we have become! No, Miss Kerrigan. You cannot use official Privy Council manpower or resources. However," he said and leaned forward, the corner of his mouth twitching, "you are literally living in the stronghold of the next generation. The greatest convergence of tatù power in the history of the world." His eyes glanced at Devon and then back to Rae. "Why not use it?"

Rae's mind flashed back to the girl, Ellie, from the library and she flashed Devon a dubious look. "They're just kids." Hadn't she just been one of them a couple years ago? "I mean, what can they really do?"

This time, both Beth and Carter laughed in unison. "They're just kids..." Beth repeated with a smile.

"Miss Kerrigan," Carter tried to restrain his amusement, "lest you forget, you are also just a kid. Both you and Devon are teenagers—yet highly trained operatives who have proven yourselves worthy time and time again."

Despite the present circumstance, Rae couldn't help but swell with pride at the words. Carter didn't give compliments out easy.

Carter pressed his fingers together as his elbows rested on his desk. "The students here at Guilder may be young and inexperienced, but they're powerful and a force in their own right. Work with them. Don't tell them what it's for—play it off as a mentoring position. In fact," he smiled, "think of it as your thesis paper. They can do the research on Cromfield while you and your team do the legwork."

"My team?" Rae asked. "I thought you said I didn't get a—"

"As far as I recall, you and Devon, though capable agents, are still on probation," Carter said coolly. "It was also brought to my attention that both Julian and Miss Skye put in for leave this morning. Now, while I can't officially sanction a team for a mission that doesn't officially exist...I can suggest you spend some quality time with your friends, can't I?"

Rae stared at him, shocked. He had been hard, almost cruel her first year. He'd changed so much. Over the last few days, Carter had come to surprise her again and again, but this was in a league of its own. It was the very reason why he was continuing to enforce their suspension, she realized. Any other agent would have been cleared the second their hunch was proven correct, but Carter was keeping her and Devon purposely on the sidelines. Smart man.

"I..." Words failed her and she bowed her head, trying not to smile. "I'll most definitely do that, sir."

"Good!" Carter clapped his hands in a business-like way. "Then I think we're done here."

Devon and Beth stood, but Rae stayed behind. "Sir, one more thing. My mother. I'd like to know what kind of protection she's—"

"*I* am protecting her."

Under any other circumstance, Rae might have talked back. But one look in Carter's eyes was enough to assure her. He had this. If Jennifer Jones herself came knocking down the gates, Rae believed Carter would send her straight down to hell.

"Good to know, sir." She followed Devon to the door before whirling around once more. "Actually, I've one more thing."

Carter sighed in exasperation. "What is it now, Miss Kerrigan?"

"I'd like to get permission to go to the hospital today to visit Luke."

Carter's face softened sympathetically. While Devon flashed her a quick look, his eyes cleared immediately and she couldn't read his expression.

Carter pulled out his phone and began tapping on it. "Of course you may. Send him our best."

Once outside, Beth hugged Rae. "I need to get going. Your Uncle Argyle's landing in a few hours and Carter has two agents escorting me to the airport to pick him up." She gave Rae a kiss on the cheek. "Let's do dinner tomorrow."

"Sounds like a plan." Rae smiled.

Beth hugged her once more before leaving her and Devon standing alone in the bright sunlight drenching the lawns.

Devon squinted towards the parking lot. "You need a ride?"

"Uh, no, I don't think so." Rae pawed the ground nervously with her shoe. "He's still really weak coming out of the coma and I don't want to—"

"Hey, I get it." He flashed her a pearly smile and tossed her his keys. "Tell him hi for me."

Rae looked at him doubtfully and he gently took her hand.

"I'm serious," he said softly. "It's because of him you have your mother back. He changed your life in a profound, permanent way for the better and I'm not blind to that. He'll always have my thanks."

Rae blinked, overwhelmed and ridiculously grateful for the maturity of that attitude, before stretching up on her toes to give him a swift kiss on the cheek. "Thanks," she said quietly. "I won't be long. See you back here tonight?"

"Count on it." He grinned. "Drive careful."

"Ha ha." She knew he was teasing about her driving skills.

An hour and a half later, and Devon's car still in one piece without a scratch on it, Rae stood outside the door to Luke's room, half wishing she was invisible. What did you say to the guy who almost died trying to reunite you with your family? How did you greet someone who just got out of brain surgery because your mentor bashed him over the head?

A doctor walked by curiously and Rae quickly whipped out her phone and pretended to be texting. She flashed him a smile as he walked past, then slipped the phone back into her pocket and stared helplessly at the door. She almost wished he had sent her away to 'let him get some rest'. She should have waited till the end of the school day, and mistakenly come after visiting hours were over.

"Rae?"

Rae jumped, almost hitting her head on the ceiling from Devon's tatù. She squinted incredulously through the fogged window.

Luke was just a normal guy. He didn't have any supernatural ability. How the hell did he know she was there?

"Are you going to stand out there all day, or do you think you might come in and talk to me?"

Blushing fire-engine red, she pushed open the door and walked sheepishly inside. Luke didn't look as bad as she thought he would, especially considering he'd just woken up from a coma. There was still a bit too much medical machinery for her liking and he still had an IV shoved in his arm, but other than that, he looked relatively normal. Only the dark circles under his eyes betrayed what had happened. That, and the fact that they'd shaved off half of his hair. "Hey," she said in a rusty voice and cleared her throat. "Hey, Luke." Her eyes dropped to the floor in shame.

"Rae! It's great to see you." The happiness in his voice made her head pop up. He greeted her with a bright, astonishing smile.

Her heart began tentatively beating for what felt like the first time in hours. Could it possibly be that he didn't vehemently despise her?

"You see that weird, paned glass on the windows?" he asked. She nodded. "It's a new thing they're trying. I can see out, but people can't see in. It's supposed to make me feel connected while providing some sense of privacy." His eyes twinkled. "It's how I saw you lurking. When'd you turn into a peeping Tom crazy person?"

She laughed at his teasing, starting to relax. "I didn't mean to lurk, I just didn't know how to...what to say." She sighed.

"Hey, come here."

She perched obediently on the bed and he took her hand in his own. "No apologies, okay?" Luke smiled. "I don't know what exactly you're thinking, or what weird sense of guilt you've been carrying around with you, but it's fine, okay?"

Maybe he'd hit his head even harder than she'd thought. "Luke, you had to have *brain surgery* because of me! That's worth an apology. And, like, a lifetime's supply of ice cream, and chocolates, and whatever else you want."

He chuckled softly and touched the side of his head before dropping his hand. "As great as that sounds, it's not exactly the case. I had to have brain surgery, because a rogue agent went nuts and hit me over the head after I uncovered some sensitive information. Info that would be useful to both our organizations." He couldn't really move too fluidly yet, but it looked like he might have shrugged. "Rae, this is what I signed up for."

She shook her head firmly, unwilling to be forgiven so easily. "You uncovered that information for me. It wasn't agency-sensitive. It was a personal favor." Her eyes flickered over the tubes and wires still holding him to the bed and her eyes filled with guilty tears. "I'll never forgive myself. You shouldn't either. I'm a Kerrigan." She hated her last name and the responsibilities that came with it.

His hand came up and weakly squeezed her shoulder. "No, no, no! None of that. You're not the one who gets to feel sorry for yourself! Look at this wicked haircut! It's boss!"

She snorted in laughter and ran her fingers along the shaven edge. "It's very modern," she said helpfully, tilting her head to see both sides of his head. "Kind of a Jekyll and Hyde sort of thing."

He laughed and reached up to touch it again. "Don't lie to me. The nurses have been hiding all mirrors, but I managed to catch my reflection in one of their reading glasses. It's pretty awful."

"Nonsense!" Rae exclaimed. "A little duct tape here, a little wig there, you'll be right as rain!"

His eyes sparkled as he tried to hit her with one of his pillows. "Very funny. At least Molly promised to help me fix it. Said she could turn it into some sort of cool mohawk."

Rae leaned back and blinked. "Molly was here?"

For whatever reason, Luke suddenly couldn't meet her gaze. "Uh, yeah. She was here when I woke up, and she stopped by earlier this morning to see how I was doing. She's pretty. I mean, she's pretty sweet!" He fidgeted. "Considering I look like Dr. Jekyll and all."

A warm flush lit Rae from head to toe. She knew that look, all too well. The only reason Molly wouldn't tell her she was coming to the hospital was if there was something a little more to it than just a regular visit.

Rae bit back a smile and nodded casually. "Yeah, Molls is the best. I really don't know where I'd be without her." Something Luke said echoed back to her. "Wait. You said Molly was here when you woke up? What about Devon?"

"He was here too," Luke assured her. "He was just down getting coffee, came back in a few minutes later." He shifted restlessly against the pillows. "Actually, the nurses told me he never left the room, even after he donated almost half his blood."

"Pardon?" Rae blanched and wondered how to move forward, but before she could say a thing, Luke held up his hand and stopped her.

"Hey—I get it. It's no big deal. I figure if a guy would be willing to virtually exsanguinate himself for another guy on behalf of some girl. Well, that's something I don't want to get in between. Not to mention I, uh," he said and cleared his throat, "I heard you two when I got to Heath Hall."

Rae closed her eyes, wishing the floor would open up and swallow her whole. "You...um, you heard that?" She did not want to have this freakin' conversation. Her cheeks burned from the heat inching its way over her scalp now too.

He looked at her speculatively for a long moment, before his face cleared with an honest smile. "It's no big deal. You didn't know I'd be coming. Plus," he said and hesitated a moment before continuing, "it's almost a relief in a way. No more passive aggressive competition with your boyfriend. No more stalking you through your files." He chuckled. "I'm kidding on that! You and me, we're meant to be friends. I'm cool with that if you are."

It was that simple? This easy? Rae reached down and squeezed his hand gently. "You're an incredible friend. I can't believe the risks you took for me. I want you to know I appreciate it from the bottom of my heart. If there's ever anything I can do to repay you, just say the word."

"Well," he grinned mischievously, "you could put in a good word for me with Molls." He looked at her face and backtracked quickly. "I mean, if that isn't too weird or anything..."

"No, no!" Rae said and bit her lip when his eyes went wide. "I mean, not no! No, it isn't weird, not no I won't put a good word in for you." She sounded like Molly now. She sighed and tried again. "It's fine! Actually, it's better than fine." Two of her favorite people in the world? What better match could there be? "I have to warn you though, most of the people who cross Molls the wrong way, end up with a few thousand volts of electricity running through their chest. Proceed with caution."

He grinned. "Duly noted." Then his face got serious. "Now, about that address I gave you. Please tell me it led to something?"

Rae jumped off the bed and began pacing in excitement. "Someone, actually. Someone who's going to want to meet you the moment you're feeling up to it."

"You found her! You found your mom?" Luke's head fell back against the pillow in relief. "I'm so happy for you."

Rae glanced back up at the wires connecting him to a heart monitor and shook her head. She couldn't help but grin. "You are truly the strangest, most selfless person I've ever met."

Luke winked at her. "Yeah, well, I've recently just found out I have a whole lot of time on my hands. Brain injury, they say. So, if you've got time, want to fill me in on what happened?"

She had all the time in the world today. Rae gave him the entire story—sparing no detail, holding no punches. He soaked it in as hungrily as someone might if they were looking forward to the next few weeks being chained to a hospital bed. When she was finished, they laughed and talked and joked around until a nurse came to banish her so that they could run a few more standard tests.

Rae kissed Luke on the forehead and headed back to Guilder feeling like a literal weight had been lifted from her chest. Leave it to Luke to find a way to cheer her up from a hospital bed.

She was still grinning to herself when she got back to Aumbry House and pushed open the door of her room. Half a dozen faces sat staring back at her.

"What the hell?" She had almost zapped everyone using Molly's tatù. She managed to catch herself in time and gazed around in confusion at the scene before her. Her room had been transformed into a virtual study center. Four extra laptops were positioned on the bed, and a literal mountain of books and documents was stacked on her dresser and in massive piles on the floor. For good measure, Molly had even dragged her desk inside from across the hall.

Rae's gaze fell directly on Molly, who looked up at her in wide-eyed panic.

"We've got a problem. A big one."

Chapter 3

"What is it?" Rae felt a tingling in her spine as she tried to sense the danger lurking around them. Her tatù tried to find the ability she had which would be the strongest and most efficient. Rae mentally focused and controlled it. There was no way Carter would have contacted Molly to put together students to help search for Cromfield. He'd have left that for Rae to sort and decide, right?

"Finals. We have finals."

For once, it wasn't about the world ending. It wasn't about psychotic serial killers, or brain washing devices, or attempts on the Royal Family. It was about something far, far worse... finals.

"Rae!" A tall blond-haired, brown-eyed girl swept past her in a small gust of wind. "Nice to see you again, Rae. Keeping out of trouble?"

Rae blinked in astonishment. What the heck was Haley doing in her room? But as she gazed around the makeshift study center, she saw that her old 'fr-enemy' was hardly the only familiar face.

"Andy? Rob?" Rae exclaimed. "Is that you?"

In a second, she pounced on both of them, taking care to brush up against their bare skin, especially Rob.

He caught the gesture with a grin and squeezed her hand. "Somebody caught the flying bug, did they?"

"What can I say?" She felt almost breathless with the rush as the familiar tatù hummed along her fingers before blending seamlessly with the others. "It's come in handy more than once. There's really nothing like it!"

"Oh, yeah?" Andy countered. "And how about mine?" He reached out and took her wrist.

All at once, a new humming joined in with the others. Rae closed her eyes for a moment as she focused on the sensation. There was something more primal about this one than the others. Something a bit more raw—untamed. Truth be told, Rae had never used Andy's tatù before, although she had always been curious. He was a bit like Rob in that he was a shifter. But instead of shifting into an eagle, he turned into a wolf.

"That's pretty intense," she murmured, ignoring her sudden craving for bloody steak. "So, where on earth have you two been? It's like you just vanished from Guilder!"

"You're one to talk!" Andy laughed.

"Yeah, overall we've been here more than you," Rob added. "The PC paired us up and sent us off to..." His voice trailed off as he glanced around the room. "Well, needless to say, somewhere really freaking cold—and we're glad to be back in England."

"It was Serbia," Andy blurted, hardly bothering to lower his voice.

Rob smacked him upside the head. "Andrew!"

Andy shrugged carelessly. "Who the hell cares? It's Rae. Plus, we're back at freaking headquarters—where could we be more safe?"

"You can never be too careful." Rae shook her head, but couldn't resist a grin. She'd forgotten how contagiously lively the young wolf could be. "I'm glad you guys are back. I really missed you!"

Rob gestured around the room with a sigh. "Well, we couldn't miss this, could we? Not that we didn't try..."

Andy frowned. "Honestly. You'd think the Privy Council would wait to sweep us away until we'd actually graduated. I'm sure I've forgotten half the stuff we were learning, and now, suddenly, we're supposed to be tested on it? I'm going to fail for sure! And then what?"

"No more Serbia," Rae said helpfully.

He shot her a rueful grin and smacked her shoulder. "Wouldn't you like that? Then you, Devon, and Julian would have no competition for the PC's new golden boys." When Rae hit him in the chest he added, "And girl."

"Oh, Rae's nobody's golden girl," Haley joined the conversation with a smirk. "She's on probation."

The boys turned back to her in surprise, but Rae narrowed her eyes suspiciously. "How do you know that?"

'Haley's the PC's secretary. She didn't pass the qualifications to be a field agent, so they have her making schedules and running files...'

Most people would have jumped out of their skin to hear a sudden voice in their head, but Rae whirled around in anticipation. Sure enough, there was Maria, nestled on the ground next to a desk with her head in a book. She glanced up and flashed Rae a huge smile.

"You're back!" Rae ditched the other three and knelt down on the floor beside her. She leaned over and hugged her before sitting back. After her initial excitement to see her friend, her face clouded in concern. "How are you feeling?"

Maria had been the first casualty of Rae's father's brainwashing device. Well, not the first—Rae's own mother was the first—but the most recent. The last time Rae had seen her, she was under heavy sedation, still spitting in rage and screaming into Carter's mind as he tried to interrogate her. Perhaps more importantly, the last time Rae saw her, she'd been attempting to kidnap the future Queen of England. Not of her own volition, of course, but Rae wasn't sure how much that would matter to a royal jury. "You're not, like, in a ton of trouble, are you?" she asked, lowering her voice.

For a second, Maria's little face clouded. "No. They understood I wasn't myself. That I wasn't in my right mind." She smiled and shrugged. "Apparently, no permanent damage was done."

"That's good." Rae watched Maria's face and pressed her eyebrows together when her friend didn't smile.

"But, I'm afraid, I'm off field work for a while."

Rae frowned indignantly. "That's so unfair! They said it themselves, you weren't in your right mind. *You* were the victim. They're just lucky it didn't happen to one of them!"

"No, you misunderstand me." Maria put her hand on Rae with a steadying smile. "I asked for a leave of absence. I needed to...clear my head. Get back to school for a while." She winced as she held up her book. "Of course, I didn't know I was coming back in time for this."

"Which brings us back to the point, people!" Molly shrieked loud enough to quiet the room. She was perched on top of a stack of mathematic textbooks, holding a cup of coffee in one hand and a paper bag in the other. Every few seconds, she rotated between the two—simultaneously drowning herself in caffeine and hyperventilating into the bag. "We've got less than three months to catch up with what we missed or it's bye-bye Privy Council, no more graduation. And I, for one, don't want to stay here another year. Now let's focus!"

"Some of us have been here!" somebody called from the other side of the room.

"Lucky you," Andy scoffed. "Some of us thought we'd already graduated and just found out the PC created a new requirement that you need to graduate high school in order to get paid."

Rae scratched her head. "I thought you had graduated."

"So did I!" Andy shook his head. "Apparently, since we didn't sit and write our final exams we are not considered high school scholars." He pointed to the textbooks by him. "Like cramming all this in is going to help us in a life and death situation where I have to shift. They don't teach that shit in textbooks!"

Rob laughed. "Headmaster Lanford did. He believed all..." He stopped talking when the room went instantly into a hushed silence. With big eyes, Rob turned to Rae. "I'm so sorry! I didn't mean... I just..."

Rae rested her hand on his forearm. "It's okay, Rob. He was around here for your schooling. I get it. It's not a big deal." She had visions of Lanford. How much she had trusted him and how she hadn't seen his betrayal coming. Imagine he was alive? The thought made her shudder. Bad people were supposed to give off evil vibes, not make you trust them and respect them.

It didn't take long for Molly to stomp her foot and get everyone's attention again. She sucked from the bag and then the coffee as her panic spread to the rest of the group, even Rae settled down with a textbook.

For the next few hours, nobody said a word except what had been taught at Guilder the past year as they submerged themselves in old lecture notes and study sheets. The final exams were notoriously difficult, and this graduating class was woefully behind. That being said, they did have one or two tricks up their sleeves, and maybe a tatù or two.

"Thank the heavens! Nicholas!"

Rae's head shot up with the rest as Nicholas MacGyver entered the room.

Nic looked around in surprise at the new set-up and straightened his glasses before they could fall off his nose. "What's going on guys? I just came by to say hi to Rae and Molly." His face brightened hopefully. "Are you guys working on something?"

Molly rolled her eyes and with a grin she teased, "For the smartest person in the world, you sure have a knack for stating the obvious."

Rae got to her feet in relief, walked straight up to MacGyver, and clapped him deliberately on the shoulder. "Good to see you, Nic." She grinned as the familiar tatù coursed back through her veins. "Well, I'm good! Anybody up for a bit of sparring?"

"Rae Kerrigan! That's not fair—that's cheating!" Molly shrieked in jealous dismay.

Rae shrugged, unable to keep the giggles inside of her contained. "I can't help it if I now have a photographic memory." She and MacGyver shared a conspiratorial grin. Nic had a particular set of skills, and his photographic memory came in handy with his tatù. Actually, it was part of his tatù. "I'll look through this stuff tonight and be ready by tomorrow. Good luck studying, guys!"

Rob and Andy got to their feet at once, followed quickly by Haley and Maria.

"We need a break! At least I do," Andy declared. "If I read anymore I think my eyes are going to start bleeding."

"Molls..." Rae said imploringly. Her redheaded friend was now the only one not leaving the room, and was staring back at the departing group in obvious distress. "Want to blow off a little steam? Maybe shock the living hell out of a few of our dear friends? That always cheers you up."

Molly looked comically back and forth between her friends and the textbooks. "But...we have so much to do! I don't think we—"

Andy and Rob marched straight back inside and picked her up by the arms, carrying her out with the rest of them. The boys were so tall that it didn't matter she was running with her feet in the air.

Her shouts of protest, however, could be heard all the way across campus. "Put me down! We have work to do! I don't want to zap you but I will. Don't you pretend you can't hear me! I see you smiling Andy! Do you want me to call your mother?! I'll tell her it's you clogging the shower drain with all your wolf hair! You two put me down!"

The girl didn't even stop to take a breath as she continued.

Nic stepped in front when Andy and Rob dropped her suddenly. Both of them shook their hands, obviously trying to get rid of the shocked feeling in their arms. MacGyver held out his hand. "Look, Molly," he assured her, "I promise I'll draw up some study sheets for you, all right? I've already gone through the database and researched every finals question each teacher has ever asked. We're all going to breeze right through."

Molly—and the rest of the gang, for that matter—cheered up considerably at Nic's comment. Everyone agreed to head off to the Oratory to spar. Someone suggested a knock out competition and Rae laughed when the boys jumped at the chance. It felt like first year all over again, without the stress of not knowing her tatù and no one judging her this year.

She led the pack, pleased with the success of her mutiny and ready to test everyone's skills against hers. When she opened the main door, she ran right into a very sweaty, and very sexy-looking Devon.

"Woah there!" He caught her as she fell back. She'd already switched her tatù to catch herself, but she didn't stop him from reaching out to touch her. "You should be more careful where you're going, Miss Kerrigan. Wouldn't want you to give anyone the wrong idea." He winked.

She pulled herself away with an incriminating blush. "Sorry. We're in a bit of a rush." Tonight, she and her boyfriend were going to have a serious talk as to the meaning of the word 'discreet'.

"What are you guys up to?" he asked with a grin, his face lighting up when he saw Andy, Rob and Nic. "Dudes!" After high-fiving them, he turned back to Rae. "I thought Molly had you all locked away studying for the next few months."

"We happen to be taking a much needed study break." Molly sniffed self-righteously. "Besides, we have something that you and your cronies didn't have for your final exams." She turned and patted Nic on the head like he was a prized collector's item. "We have MacGyver."

Julian appeared behind Devon, running his hands back through his long dark hair and securing it in what Rae thought to be a very 'pirate-looking' ponytail. His muscles glistened with sweat as it was clear both he and Devon had just been sparring themselves, and the thin tanks and low jeans both guys were wearing offered the crowd a rather tantalizing look at their rather delicious physiques.

"Aw, you don't think we too stole Nic when it was time for our own exams? His brilliance isn't just contained to your generation," Julian teased.

There was a small cut just within his hairline that was dripping a slow line of blood down to his ear. The second she saw it, Haley stepped forward with a seductive smile. "You're hurt! Here, let me help you with that."

He braced himself automatically against her advances and shook his head politely. "Oh, that's sweet, but I got it. Thanks."

"You sure, Julian?" Rae teased back. She knew how her best friend still grew uncomfortable by the constant stream of female attention he got. He stood out with his good looks, but he was shy. Haley definitely didn't seem his type. "It looks pretty bad."

Devon glanced over with an unconcerned grin. "Doesn't look that bad to me. Sorry though, man. Must have caught you with that spear."

Julian raised his eyebrows, wincing for a mere split second before hiding it. "You mean that spear you launched at my head while I was texting? Not exactly fair play."

Devon's eyes sparkled. "Well, maybe if you weren't so caught up with the texting, you would've seen it coming. Come to think of it, who was distracting you so much? Rae?" He turned to her. "Did you get a text from Julian today?"

Rae shook her head with a scarcely contained smile. "Nope, not me."

"Hmm." Devon looked around with a mock frown. "Molls?"

"Wasn't me either." She grinned, playing along.

Devon's handsome face came up blank. "And it obviously wasn't me, I was the one throwing the spear. So, whosoever could it—"

"I'd be less concerned with your friend's texting habits than with the fact that you launched a spear at his head."

Every head swiveled around as Alecia walked into the Oratory.

"Hey there!" Rae smiled, forgetting to continue teasing Julian. Just as Rae and some of the others had working internships with the Privy Council, Alecia had one with one of the biggest hospitals in London. The same one where Luke was presently recovering. Her gift made her a natural fit. She was a brilliant diagnostician and a healer. "Didn't see you this morning at the hospital. How's Luke doing?"

"I was packing," she replied. "Apparently, me and everyone else with an acting internship is being pulled back to Guilder for final exams. Why would they do that now? It's not like it's going to change our jobs." She rolled her eyes as if she couldn't care less about whatever standardized testing the school had in mind. "But Luke's doing well. They're actually releasing him tomorrow. He just found out about a bit ago." She glanced around. "I thought Molly would've told you."

Molly blushed a million shades of crimson, but Rae kept her reproach to herself, biting her tongue with a little grin. "Well, we were all studying, but we came here for a little sparring break."

"I can see that," she said, looking at Julian. "That's not deep, but you're going to want to clean it out with some antiseptic."

He smiled and backed further away from Haley as she moved incredibly close to him. "Will do."

"In the meantime," Rae gestured to inside the Oratory, "how about we all do some sparring?"

"*Actually*," Devon put his hand around her shoulders and guided her back out towards the door, "me and Julian were just coming to get you and Molls. Apparently, you two are starting your mentorship program today. Carter set up a meeting in the library for you to meet the troops."

Rae's eyes drifted mournfully back to the practice arena, where her friends were already starting to yank out some of her favorite weapons and toys. "Right now?" She knew Carter was doing this to give them a full spectrum of tatùs, but a little sparring couldn't hurt.

"Hey," Devon grinned, "eyes front, Kerrigan. You and Miss Skye over there are tragically behind on your community service hours—which you also need to graduate." He lowered his voice a couple decibels. "And you and I know there's a lot more to this than just mentoring..."

Rae nodded and waved goodbye to her friends as the four of them headed back out into the late afternoon sun. The sounds of laughter and playful screams echoed back to them and she couldn't help but smile. While the prospect of final exams sounded terrible, she was almost glad the school had pulled everybody back. For once, they all got to be kids again. Of course, it was bittersweet as the school portion of their lives was officially ending. Over the years, Rae had come to understand that the secret world of tatùs was very closely intertwined. Devon and Julian were still living on school grounds for this year, just to be closer to headquarters, and most all the people in her graduating class would be going to live in the same area as they all worked for variations of the same company. One way or another, for better or worse, they were all stuck with each other.

Aside from Haley, Rae couldn't have asked for a better group of friends. Which also meant a strong group of tatùs to work with to solve the mystery behind Cromfield.

Speaking of friends, she turned to Molly, Devon, and Julian with a frown. "So, what exactly are we supposed to be doing with this mentorship program?"

"Today is just a meet and greet," Devon assured her. "We're going to scope out the new abilities and get a better idea of who we're going to be working with to find Cromfield."

Julian elbowed her with a purposeful nudge. "We're going to want you to shake a lot of hands, if you know what I mean."

"Without permission?" Rae asked uncomfortably.

"I'm sure they all know what you can do. It's up to them," Devon said lightly. "But at the same time, you're going to be mentoring them for this first year of school. The year they're coming into their powers. I can't see why anyone wouldn't want a personal self-help guide to their tatù."

They had reached the library and Devon and Molly strode in with confidence. Rae, however, lingered outside on the steps.

After glancing ahead, Julian turned and hung back with her. "What's the matter?" he asked with a soft smile. "Afraid they'll think you bite?"

Rae smiled back, but she couldn't hide the worry from her eyes. "It's not that..." Her voice dropped down to a whisper, "The last time I involved someone in my plans, they ended up in a coma. Not quite sure I'm ready to repeat the mistake."

Julian put his arm gently around her shoulder. "And he woke up." Rae let her eyes flicker up to his face, and he gave her a sad half-smile. "It's the world we live in, Rae. Bad things happen. All we can do is prepare the best we can to be ready for what's to come." He nodded towards the library. "And these kids deserve that chance too. They deserve to have someone guide them into their powers. They deserve the chance to grow up in a world without Cromfield."

Rae drew in a shuddering breath, but nodded. He was right. As usual.

She flashed him a smile, and together, they headed inside. The Tudor-carved walls off the hallway were brightly lit with old stained glass lamps and their quiet footsteps were dampened by the old marble black-and-white flooring that covered most of the buildings at Guilder. They walked quietly to the large study room that the new students were waiting in. Rae hadn't been in this library much. She spent most of her time in the library at Aumbry House and she marveled at the detail in the wood carvings so similar to those in the Oratory. She ran her fingers over one picture and wondered briefly if there were hidden doors in this building like those in the Oratory. It looked so similar.

Julian paused outside the door where noise and chatter seemed to bounce off on the other side. "You ready?" He smiled encouragingly. "It's just like any other Privy Council job, you just get to work with kids instead of miserable adults." He chuckled and winked at her as he turned the knob and opened the door.

She nodded and took a deep breath.

The second they entered the room, the kids gathered inside suddenly fell silent. You could have heard a pin drop as they stared wide-eyed towards the door.

Rae fought the urge to roll her eyes, and took a deliberate step away from Julian. She bet they weren't looking at him. "Yes, that's right. I'm Rae Kerrigan. Daughter of the famed lunatic, Simon Kerrigan. Take a look, feel free to stare." She smiled despite trying to sound sarcastic. Several kids had the decency to glance down or away, but most of them stared wide-eyed at her. "I'm currently the only known person in the world to have two original tatùs." She ran her gaze across the room and lowered her voice, nearly laughing when the kids leaned forward as one to hear what she was going to say. "And if any of you touch me, I'll be able to mimic your tatù also."

Even Molly was leaning forward as she stood beside Devon. Rae saw Devon cover his mouth and tried to hide his laughter with a cough.

Rae moved to walk toward them. "Rest assured, I am not my father. I'm a student here at Guilder just like you. In fact, I barely knew my father, and have worked tirelessly since I got here to try and undo whatever damage he caused. I'm an agent for the Privy

Council, and both they and the school, have trusted me enough to appoint me and my friend Molly here to be your mentors. We are not here to judge you or boss you around. We're here to help. Right, Molls?"

Molly looked at her with wide eyes, like she was one of the students as well. She blinked suddenly and jumped up. "Yes! We're here to help! Rae's not scary. She was my roommate our first year here and even then she didn't scare me. She's a freak."

"Molly!" Devon exclaimed.

Molly looked at him and shrugged. "What? Aren't we all?" She turned back to the group of kids, raising her hand and snapping her fingers so little blue sparks flicked from them. "I can make electricity. I also have an amazing fashion sense." She frowned a moment. "I see a lot of you here could use more help in that department."

Julian stepped forward and put his hand on Molly's wrist, dropping her hand down. "Thanks, Molly."

A boy near the back cleared his throat. "Kerrigan! Can you do what she just did?"

"Yup." Rae raised her hand and mimicked Molly's sparks.

"Sheesh!" The younger boy shook his head and muttered, "You friggin' are Simon Kerrigan's kid. My father said you were just like him."

Rae's tatù automatically switched to Devon's ability so she could hear what he said. "You're a boy," she said to him, emphasizing the word boy, "why haven't you been to Guilder sooner?" She didn't wait for him to answer before continuing, "If anyone has a problem with me—there's the door." She waited for the judgmental boy to get up and leave, and probably half the class. No one did. "Well then, shall we get started?" She extended her hand.

The reaction wasn't as instant as she was hoping. In fact, most of the teenagers held back until Devon stepped forward and started moving around the room and started shaking their hands.

He showed them his tatù and openly talked about it. He was good. Really good.

Eventually, everyone came up and introduced themselves to Rae, with most shaking her hand.

Everyone...except one.

"You told me never to shake hands, remember?"

Rae looked down to see a pair of fiery green eyes staring back at her. She had to admire the girl's pluck. She was smaller than most armoires, but still, she held her ground.

"Ellie!" Rae racked her brain for the girl's name and nearly shouted it when she remembered. "I'm glad to see you again. I wanted to apologize." She shifted uncomfortably. "You caught me...well, let's just say you caught me on a bad day. I didn't mean to snap at you, especially when you were just being friendly. I'm sorry. I'm not usually like that." For a minute she thought about her mentioning that she wasn't her father. Ellie probably believed she was her father. "I'm really sorry."

Ellie held her gaze for a moment before her face softened into a smile. "It's okay. I figured you were in the middle of something—you were covered in blood after all."

Rae shook her head with a grin. "I'm afraid you'll find that's actually pretty normal for me."

"Being covered in blood?"

Rae laughed. "Sometimes. But I meant that I'm always in the middle of something."

Devon laughed suddenly from the other side of the room. "Rae's a bit of a multitasker," he called out to them.

The girl giggled. "Anyway, there's no use shaking my hand. I don't have my tatù yet." She stared around the room with a longing jealousy.

Rae felt an instant protective kinship rise up within her. She hadn't turned sixteen yet when she first started at Guilder either. She knew exactly how hard it could be. "That's okay." She threw her arm around the girl's thick cardigan with a smile. "You know...I was a bit late coming to the party myself, and now look at me. It all turned out okay. Molly had it too. She got hers not long after school started."

Ellie looked distinctly troubled for a moment, before deliberately clearing her face to a grin.

Great job, Rae. Tell her that you're a blood-covered daughter of a madman, then say—don't worry! You can grow up to be just like me! Or Chatty-Kathy Molly! "Anyway..." Rae hurried to move on. "I'm looking forward to working with you."

"Me, too." Ellie still looked nervous.

Rae decided to give her some space and asked Devon to help Ellie with any questions she might have about Guilder that Rae couldn't answer. She figured it would give the young girl a chance to gaze at the handsome Devon Wardell and space from Rae.

She moved a few steps away and gazed around the room. She had to admit, she was surprisingly encouraged by the talent she found there. There was Caleb, a boy who could control anything liquid. Felecia, a girl with x-ray vision, who seemed to find Devon and Julian most appealing. Emme, whose unique dolphin tatù allowed her to breathe underwater. And then there was Ethan, nicknamed 'Dollar Bill'. His ability allowed him to make anything he wanted appear at random.

As Rae felt the new tatùs coursing through her blood, she was especially excited to try out Dollar Bill's. She couldn't even begin to imagine how often it would come in handy.

In fact, she was just testing it out, trying to produce some candy to hand out to the rest of the kids, when Julian called, "Hey Rae—you're going to want to check this one out!"

Rae walked over to him and Devon, who were standing next to a tall girl with sheets of raven-black hair. The girl smiled shyly and extended her hand as Devon made the introductions.

"Rae, meet Cassidy. Cassidy—Rae." He grinned as they shook hands. "Our new friend Cassidy here has a rather coveted ability. You see, the skull means that she can actually—"

"Holy hand grenades! You can turn invisible!"

The room burst out laughing as Rae held her arm up in front of her and watched it slowly fade away. It had been a long-standing Guilder joke that they'd yet to meet anyone who could actually disappear into thin air. It was a tatù Rae had been itching to get her hands on since she'd learned there were tatùs in the first place. She felt like Harry Potter and the invisibility cloak, except she didn't need the cloak.

"This is awesome!" She grinned as the other side of her body vanished into the air.

Cassidy's eyes grew wide. "How can you do that so quickly? I can only fade out my hands, and that alone takes a whole lot of concentration, followed by a massive headache."

Rae smiled as she popped back into view. "I've been working at trying out multiple tatùs for quite a while."

Devon chuckled and elbowed her. "Rae's got a natural knack for figuring tatùs out. Faster than most people." He shook his head and gazed at her with adoring eyes. "She's pretty amazing."

He and Rae stood staring at each other with silly smiles on their faces until Julian cleared his throat loudly.

Rae blinked and gave her head a shake. "So, yeah, that's why I'm here," she said loudly, trying to address the whole class. "The four of us were in your shoes just a few years ago, and our abilities have already come into their own. Pretty much. We're always learning and, apparently, as we mature, so do our tatùs. We're here to help you learn like we did. Devon helped me. He's a great mentor." Her eyes flashed to the only person in the room not paying attention. "Molly?"

Molly looked up from the young boy standing beside her and grinned as sparks flew from both his hands. "This one's already well on his way."

Rae chuckled. Of course Molly would latch on to the one person with the same ability as she had. "And you are?"

"Noah—" the boy started to say.

But Molly cut him off, patting him indulgently on the head. "We'll call him...Protégé."

Devon rolled his eyes and stepped to the center of the floor. "We'll be meeting with you twice a week to see how your abilities are developing and answer any questions you may have. We'll be around on campus so feel free to talk to us anytime you need to. Next week we'll have a little research project for you guys to start working on. Not homework, but fun, cool stuff."

"Have a great week, everyone!" Molly dismissed them by the door. "Don't forget to study, study! Finals will be here before you know it!"

As the kids filed out, she turned to Rae, Devon and Julian with a wide smile. "Noah's going to be the best one in his class—I can feel it!"

Julian shook his head with a grin. "And that wouldn't have anything to do with his ability now would it?"

"Not at all!" Molly raised her head like she was offended. "I'm not tatù-prejudiced."

"Sure, sure." Rae slipped on her jacket as she glanced at the clock. "I'm having dinner with my mom and Uncle Argyle tonight. Do you guys want to come?"

Molly reached for Rae and shocked her shoulder. "Definitely! I'm starving!"

"Lead the way," Julian said as he grabbed his messenger bag.

Only Devon hesitated with a small frown. Rae slipped her hand into his and squeezed it gently. "What's the matter, babe?" She smiled, liking the nickname and knowing she couldn't use it very often in public.

He glanced around the suddenly empty library chairs. "I'm just worried."

"My Uncle Argyle's old school, but we don't have to say anything about our relationship. He's not going to quiz you or give you a hard time."

Devon waved his hand. "I'm up for food." He smiled briefly. "I'm just worried about what we're doing here. Sure, we might catch a break and pick up on Cromfield's trail, but that's only solving half our problem. If Cromfield's even out there or it's some apparition of him, we don't know." He ran his free hand through his hair. "What bothers me is that Jennifer's still out there. She knows all our secrets. What if she shares them with others? She's been with us since she was our age!"

Rae's face fell as the dilemma circled back to the forefront of her mind. They not only needed to find Jenn, but they needed to find the files she stole from Luke. They might hold the key to finally tracking down the bastard who did all this.

"Well, Jenn has a flat in the city," Julian volunteered.

Molly and Rae turned to him curiously, but Devon looked over with a sudden smile. "That's right! I'd forgotten all about that place."

"They wouldn't have searched it—"

"—they don't even know it exists."

The boys finished each other's sentences with cocky grins, and then just stood there until Molly finally stamped her foot. "Anybody want to clue me in as to what's going on?"

"Jennifer had a secret flat in the city," Devon explained, now moving to the door with a determined sense of purpose. "Kind of like a safe house. A place no one knew about where she could lay low if a mission ever went bad."

Rae raised her eyebrows dangerously. "And how do you two know about it?"

The boys shared quick looks.

"She took us there once or twice when we were working together," Julian shrugged innocently. "Nothing happened—we just needed a safe spot to kill a few hours on a mission."

"Uh-huh," Molly said with a grin.

But the information had lit the adrenaline in Rae's veins. They might catch a break. Finally, they had something that might give them the edge they needed. "That's perfect!" she exclaimed. "So, after dinner tonight?"

Devon smiled but shook his head. "It'll have to be early tomorrow morning. We'll need to take a little road trip."

"Where is this safe place?" Molly crossed her arms over her chest.

Julian and Devon grinned and said at the same time, "London."

Chapter 4

What exactly was a girl supposed to wear to her first-ever family reunion? Rae switched from one outfit, to another, to another, until she finally called Molly in a panic. She was close to tears.

"What? What's the matter?" Molly answered in a rush. "Are you hurt? Is somebody in there with you? I'm coming! What kind of voltage should I be using? It's not Carter, is it?! I always knew that guy was a sneaky little snake! Just stay calm Rae—I'll be there in a flash!"

"...need your help picking out a dress," Rae finished the sentence she'd barely started. However, the line had already gone dead. Fortunately, Rae had the good sense to duck and protect her computer, when Molly burst through the door a second later in a wave of electricity.

"Where is he?" Molly exclaimed, smoke still curling from her fingers as she searched the room. "Did I get him?"

"No, but you fried my curling iron," Rae said in dismay, holding up the smoldering remains.

Far from being apologetic, Molly looked confused. "Why did you call then? What's the trouble?"

"The *trouble* is that I don't know what I'm supposed to be wearing." Rae gestured helplessly to her closet. "Are pants to informal? Like I'm not taking it seriously? But then, is a dress too formal? Like we can't have casual family dinners because it's always going to be an *occasion*. You know, what with the brainwashing and devastating fire and all?"

Molly's eyes travelled slowly from the smoking closet back to her friend. "You're going to see your mother and uncle together for the first time in over a decade, and you're worried about what you're going to *wear?*"

Rae nodded and a happy tear slipped down her friend's face.

"Oh Rae," she beamed, "it's like we're finally on the same page!"

Forty minutes later, Molly and Rae knocked tentatively on the door to a little cottage in an unfamiliar part of campus—the faculty quarters. Both of them were wearing skirts. The door burst open a second later and Beth pulled them inside.

"Oh girls!" She gave each of them a tight hug. "I'm so glad we decided to do this tonight. My captor over here," she cast a look back inside the house and Rae was surprised to see Carter sitting on a recliner in the parlor, "decided it was too dangerous for me to go to the airport to get Argyle, so I haven't seen him yet. He's due here any minute!"

Hearing his name, Carter got up from the chair and wandered over. "I told you Beth, it just wasn't worth the risk." He smiled at her fondly before turning to greet the girls, his face no longer readable. "Miss Kerrigan. Miss Skye. How's the studying coming along?"

"Uh...it's fine." Rae glanced uneasily between him and her mother, wondering why in the world he was hovering about in Beth's house.

Molly swept in to the rescue, as tactful as ever. "What exactly are you doing here, sir? I thought this was supposed to be a *family* dinner."

Carter looked at her incredulously, but it apparently hadn't occurred to Molly for even one instant that she didn't technically fall into that category herself. Looking faintly amused, he picked up his coat and headed for the door. "Beth and I were just talking, but I'm on my way out now. I'll leave you three to it. Enjoy your time together. Tell Argyle I said hello."

Just as he reached the door, there was a knock on it. He opened it and Devon and Julian walked inside. Carter glanced from the boys to Molly, before his eyes came to rest a little accusingly on Rae.

"I can see it's not exactly a strict guest list. I thought we agreed to take things easy with Beth."

"Why don't you stay, James?" Beth asked kindly, oblivious to the sudden tension.

But at the same time, Rae called, "Have a good night, sir."

"I appreciate the offer, Beth, but I think your daughter would like some time with you. I'm sure Argyle is a nervous wreck as he has no idea what's all going on. Not exactly phone conversation. I will see you again tomorrow." Carter flashed Rae an exasperated look before waving goodbye and sweeping out the door.

"What?" Rae asked innocently when Beth stared at her. "Did you ever think maybe it's a little uncomfortable for me to have dinner with the headmaster of the school who just happens to be my boss?"

"Uh-huh," Beth said doubtfully, her eyes twinkling.

"It's also uncomfortable how he makes googly eyes at you, and he smiles all the time."

Beth touched her hair. "He does? I hadn't noticed. I've been too busy watching Devon make googly eyes at you."

"Mom!" Rae's face burned. "Tatùs don't date!"

Devon frowned from where he stood behind Beth.

"I mean the older ones, like you or Carter. It's strictly... forbidden!"

"Really?" Beth's eyebrows went up. "I'm still working on my memory and James isn't interested. He has a very serious job. He's just pleased I'm all right. That's it, Rae. You don't need to worry."

A knock on the door ended the conversation.

"That has to be him," Beth's voice fell to a whisper, "everyone else is here."

Rae shoved her forward with a little smile. "Go answer it, mom. He's dying to see you."

After smoothing down her blouse, Beth took a deep breath and pulled open the door. All the color drained from Argyle's face the moment he saw her, and for a split second, both adults just stood frozen and stared. Rae could practically hear their hearts pounding away in their chests, until Argyle finally gathered himself enough to say, "B-Bethany?"

Then they came together.

The four teenagers looked politely away as the siblings embraced for the first time in over a decade. Both had tears in their eyes, and both seemed incredibly reluctant to let go, as if worried that if they did, they might wake up and none of this would be real.

When they finally pulled back, Argyle took Beth by the shoulders, looking her up and down before saying in a hesitant voice, "Beth, my name is Argyle. I'm your, well, I'm your brother."

The emotional silence that followed was shattered by Beth's ringing laughter. "I'm pretty clear on that, thanks. But thanks for the re-introduction."

Argyle stepped back in shock. "You...you remember me? You got your memory back?"

Beth beamed at Rae proudly. "Actually, my daughter got it back for me. Just one of her many new talents. It's not all there, but the past is, and I'm piecing together the rest of the missing pieces."

"Is that right?" Argyle looked curiously at Beth before his eyes flickered over to Rae.

Rae smiled at him expectantly, but she could have sworn the faintest shadow crossed his face before he smiled back. She went over to him and hugged him as well. "It's good to see you Uncle Argyle."

"You too, lass." He smiled and stepped back to see her. "You've grown. You look more like your mother every day. Aunt Linda's sent cookies along and she misses you."

"Chocolate chip?"

He smiled. "Aye! Of course!" He leaned in and said in a lower tone, "Yer not givin' the teachers here a hard time are ya? We got a call ta say you've been pulled back to do yer exams. Probation too. At Guilder?" He set his mouth in a stern fatherly line. "Change can come in many forms in our lives. It might come forcefully like a tidal wave, or creep along incrementally like a glacier. It might come in the form of devastating tragedy, difficult choices, broken relationships, or even through new opportunities. I hope it's all working out right for you, sweetie. I really hope so."

Rae smiled. "More proverbs of truth? I haven't had one in a long time and I'm glad you're here." She hugged him again. "Thanks so much for taking care of me all these years, Uncle Argyle. I should have said it more often."

He stared at her, his eyes welling up before he suddenly cleared his throat and straightened. "Enough of this mush! Let's celebrate these new opportunities. I'm sorry I can't stay for the graduation, but Aunt Linda doesn't like being on her own too long these days."

Beth gestured them to the table. "Come, let's enjoy our time together. I have wine. Big kids can have a glass too."

The first half of the dinner conversation was almost exclusively between Beth and Argyle. Not that the kids could blame them. Actually, Rae and her friends had the time of their lives sipping wine and watching the emotional reunion, their heads whipping back and forth like a tennis match. Stories were told, memories were exchanged. At one point, Beth—eager to show off her new power—lit her entire body aflame for the entertainment of the table.

Molly, Devon, and Argyle all leapt back in surprise, but Julian just smiled at Rae as they watched Beth proudly douse the flames.

"Someone's feeling pretty lucky..." Rae murmured with a conspiratorial grin.

Julian blushed. "I drew it happening beforehand. Best to come to these things prepared."

Rae giggled and Devon reached over and squeezed her hand under the table. "What's so funny?" He shot her an indulgent grin. "You laughing because your boyfriend's not fireproof like you?" He said the words so softly that only she could hear, but she still stiffened nervously and pulled her hand away under the pretense of pouring herself another glass of wine. She hadn't even finished the first one yet.

Her uncle's eyes followed every movement, but he held his tongue until—

"So, Rae, we're coming up on your big graduation. Have you decided who you're bringing along as your date?"

Rae felt her face burn beet red, and for a moment, she wondered if her uncle had powers after all. "Um...I hadn't quite decided yet." She didn't have the courage to look at Devon and the table grew suddenly quiet.

"Because I'd love to come along as a plus one. See you walk across the stage. I had hoped to come regardless."

Rae's eyes flickered without her permission to Devon, who was frozen with his wine halfway to his lips before she gulped and looked down at her plate. "Um, yeah of course. I mean, if you're still in England. I thought you'd be flying back to New York."

Argyle's gaze fixed on Devon, who promptly drained the rest of his wine, keeping his eyes locked on the wall. "I'll fly back," he continued. "I tentatively booked the flight at the start of the school year. I think it's important to do these things right." He stressed the last words in a way that made Rae bite the inside of her cheek and Devon reach discreetly for the bottle.

"Argyle," Beth chided, "leave the girl alone. I'm sure she doesn't want to bring her uncle to her graduation. She's a kid. Let her go out and have fun."

Argyle surveyed his sister carefully before his lips thinned into a hard line. "Beth, I know you've been gone for a while, but surely you, more than anyone, know the danger of romantically involving yourself with another tatù."

There was not a sound at the little table. The entire room had gone still.

"Rae wasn't raised around these rules, but you were." Argyle spoke now to Devon, forcing him to maintain eye contact with the older man. "You should know better. If you really cared about her you would—"

"Sir, I'm sorry," Devon's face had paled but he struggled to keep his voice steady, "I really don't have any idea what—"

"Don't play that game with me, Mr. Wardell." Argyle didn't raise his voice when he got angry, instead, it lowered to a deadly calm. "I've raised Rae since she was just a child. And I'll be damned if she throws what little chance she already has away on some—"

"You may have raised her," Beth countered sharply, "but I'm her mother. If these two have genuine feelings for each other, then I see no reason to—"

"What did you mean by that?" Rae asked suddenly, directing Argyle's attention to her. "*What little chance I already have. What does that even mean?*"

Molly, Julian, and Devon kept their eyes fixed on the table, but Argyle regarded her calmly.

"You're a Kerrigan." His voice held no blame, just resignation. "In the eyes of this community, the odds are always going to be stacked against you. You, more than anyone, must follow its rules to the letter. The fact that you already have a potentially dangerous tatù—"

"Potentially dangerous tatù?" Rae's eyebrows shot up and she leaned towards her uncle.

"Please, Rae." He scoffed. "Between what I heard from the agents on the way back from the airport and what I've seen here myself, you're careening headfirst down a dangerous road and I'll be damned if I'm not going to do what I can to stop it. It's my job."

Rae's breathing had gone very shallow. She couldn't believe what she was hearing. Couldn't believe the words coming out of her own uncle's mouth. Even now, she could tell they were said out of love, familial concern, but how could he say them? She couldn't change who she was! "A dangerous road, huh?" she asked softly, her voice lowering as much as his.

"Rae, think about how this looks." He bypassed Beth and spoke directly to her. "You have the same ability as your father—which was already one of the greatest the PC had ever seen—except yours is already even more powerful. Now, on top of that, you're clearly smitten with this boy who has his own tatù." Argyle's face looked pained. "In the eyes of our world, you're starting down the exact path as Simon Kerrigan!"

"I am nothing like my father!" Rae spat. "I can't believe you would even say that!"

Argyle held up his hands. "You don't have to prove it to me, my dear Rae. I know it with all my heart. But this is the world that you're living in now, Rae. I was Simon's best friend. I believed in him, thought he was a good guy. He stole my sister, broke her heart, hurt you and for what?" Argyle tossed his napkin on the table. "He made us think Beth was dead! You don't think this boy here won't do the same? That he's sweet now and he'll never change? Never hurt you? You need to listen to me and follow—"

"No, you need to listen!" Rae pushed back her chair and stood up from the table. "Did you ever think that maybe it's a good thing how strong my tatù is, seeing how ever since I got into this *world*, people have been trying to kill me? Did you ever think for even a second, that it's natural I would get attached to the one person who's been there with me through it all—constantly risking his life to save mine?"

Argyle grew quiet, though he looked at Devon with less disdain and maybe an ounce or two of respect.

Rae wasn't finished. This was a conversation that should have been had a long time ago. "I came from two people with tatùs! How can you expect me to—"

"To what, Rae? Your mother believed Simon was good. So did I. I think Simon did as well. He believed his theories and tested limits. I see you doing the same," Argyle stressed. "Your mother was smitten with the man, but she didn't..." His voice trailed off.

"Love him?"

Both Rae and Argyle turned to the end of the table as Beth got slowly to her feet. She looked at Argyle and shook her head. "Is that what you were going to say, Argyle?" she asked quietly. "That I didn't love him? Because I did."

Argyle's face flushed, but he seemed incapable of speech. He grabbed his napkin and balled it up with his fist as he stared wordlessly at his sister.

"I didn't marry Simon for work, I did it for love." She turned to Rae. "And loving him, for however brief a time, gave me the greatest gift I could ever ask for." Her eyes hardened and returned to her brother. "How dare you chastise my daughter for falling in love. As if it's something that can be helped. As if it's something in our power to control!"

Argyle's expression grew mild in the face of her anger. "I'm only voicing my concerns. I love Rae. And now not only is there this relationship, but there's her tatù—"

"Her tatù saved my life! It got me my memory back!" Beth cried. "It brought me back to my family, Argyle, and revealed the traitor in our midst. You can't possibly begrudge her for that. If you need to place blame, place it where it belongs. It was Jennifer, not Rae, who—"

The fighting continued as Molly and Julian slowly pushed back their chairs and silently filed to the door. Devon looked at Rae with sympathetic eyes before he followed them.

Casting a look at her screaming family, Rae got up and joined them out the door.

The cold night air bit into their faces, and they stuck in a close huddle as they filed back across the lawn.

"Well, for a first family dinner that wasn't so bad," Molly said, trying to sound cheery. "Honestly, you should see my family go at it sometimes."

Julian squeezed Rae's shoulder. "They'll cool down and get over it. It's what families do."

"They both love you," Devon finished, lacing his arm around her waist and pulling her into his side. "They love you and they're worried. That's all."

Just like your dad. Strangely enough, Rae wasn't that concerned with the fight. They did love her, and they were worried about her, she knew that. What was lingering in her mind was the last thing her mother had shouted before they slipped out the door.

If you want to blame someone, blame Jennifer.

She was right. If it weren't for Jennifer's involvement, none of this would have ever happened. Cromfield would have been without a spy, and Rae could have grown up with at least one of her parents intact. She would not be under constant suspicion from the rest of the tatù community, and needless to say, this would not have been her first family dinner.

Yes, Jennifer was to blame. And while Carter assured Rae that he had forces on the ground, searching day and night, Rae knew they wouldn't find her.

She was too smart. Too quick. Too deadly. To catch a person like Jennifer, you'd need someone equally ruthless. Someone who could get inside the mind of a killer. Maybe someone who was a bit unhinged themselves.

The moment Rae's friends left her alone in her room, she leaned back against the door and pulled out her cell phone. She stared at it for a long time.

There was someone she needed to text.

Chapter 5

The next morning, Rae, Devon, Molly, and Julian were speeding down the interstate towards London in Julian's sports car. They'd left before the rest of the school had risen, hoping to get to the city before seven forty-five in the morning, which, according to Julian, was the approximate time of London's second precinct police shift change. How he knew this—no one asked. Instead, they piled into his Jaguar and hit the road with the sole purpose of breaking into the secret home of a murderous sociopath.

It was just like old times. Sort of.

"I still don't understand why we couldn't have gone during the *afternoon* shift change," Molly complained for the millionth time. "I feel like I had just shut my eyes when Mr. Bedside Manner over there," she shot a scathing look at Devon, "started pounding on my door."

Devon flashed her a grin. "What was I supposed to do? Julian texted me that he'd just drawn the scorched remains of your alarm clock."

"Oh Molls, you didn't execute, aka electra-cute, another one, did you?" Rae asked with mock concern. "That's the sixth one this month!"

"So kill me," Molly grumbled, crossing her arms petulantly across her chest as she slouched down in the seat to get a little shut-eye. "It's not my fault your crazy family kept me awake until one in the morning. I couldn't sleep when we got back. I was worried they might try and kill each other."

Rae turned to stare out at the road. Molly was right. The 'family dinner' had turned into a fighting shouting match. "It did get a little crazy."

"At least now we know where Rae gets it," Devon said with a smile as he glanced in the rearview mirror at her and winked. "The crazy, I mean."

"Hey!" She clapped his shoulder with a mild shock in her hand and smirked as he jumped and lurched the car suddenly from the movement of his hands on the steering wheel.

"Didn't anyone ever tell you not to shock the driver?" Julian said suddenly, sounding annoyed.

Devon glanced at him and pretended to rub his shoulder, sending Rae a rueful grin. "I'm good. With last night and now. Family can be a pain when they just don't get it."

"At least I'm not the one with a secret girlfriend," Rae teased Julian, suddenly feeling giddy from Devon's sweet comment.

Julian scoffed and turned to face her, the corners of his lips turning upward. "And it's only as of—what—last week that your boyfriend's no longer a secret, and in all actuality, he still technically *is* a secret. So, I wouldn't go boasting about that just yet. Look what happened last night."

Devon wound his arm back behind his chair and took her hand. "I would. Whatever it takes."

Ahhh, sweet and sexy. He was a deadly combination to love.

Julian chuckled. "Right. Especially with both of you living back at Guilder right under the nose of your—"

Devon cut him off with a sharp look, and a faint blush tinted the top of Julian's high cheekbones. Rae stared back and forth between the two.

"Right under the nose of your...what?" she demanded, although she had a sneaking suspicion she already knew who they were talking about. "Your father? Did he say something—"

"Look, we're here," Julian interjected neatly, pulling into a shady-looking alley.

"Not a moment too soon," Devon added under his breath. He jumped out of the car, using the extra speed of his tatù, and Julian was quick to follow. The girls, however, stayed in the car, casting dubious looks at their surroundings.

"This is where Jennifer made her safe house?" Molly said doubtfully. The place was littered with mold and deceased cigarette butts, and from the sounds of it, someone was vomiting back behind a dumpster. Not even a homeless animal would hang around here. "Is it even safe to leave Julian's car here?"

"He'll see ahead if it's going to be stolen, I hope." Rae popped the seat forward to get out, she didn't want to admit it looked pretty scummy. Too bad she couldn't make things invisible besides herself with that new ink. It sure would come in handy now. She looked around, feeling a bit wary before exiting the car. "Come on. Let's get this over with. We can't let the guys go in there alone. Maybe we'll get lucky and Jennifer's here. We can catch her and slap the cuffs on her."

"We don't even have cuffs." Molly sighed and pushed the car seat forward to get out of the back on her side. "Good thing I didn't wear my nice shoes..."

They cautiously followed Devon and Julian into the smelly building. They stayed near the walls, just not close enough to touch them. Molly's sounds of disgust would give Jenn ample time to let her know they were coming.

Devon kicked in the door. He and Julian moved inside the room with skilled precision. They moved as a team and Rae could see why Carter kept the two of them working together, they knew how to back each other up and move as one, without even having to communicate.

Not surprising, no one came into the hall to check the noise or why a door to another apartment had been kicked in. Molly and Rae walked into the apartment at the same time and got stuck for a moment in the doorway. Rae turned sideways so Molly could get through and she covered the rear. She needed to start focusing on the job at hand, not act like the silly girlfriend along for the ride. She had skills and she knew how to use them.

Except Jennifer's safe house was more like a dingy one-room studio. There was a mattress shoved into one corner, no blankets or pillows, and a broken mini-fridge shoved into the other.

Rae sighed, clearly disappointed. "What a complete waste of time." She could catalogue everything inside the room in a single sweep.

Devon moved to the dirty kitchen counter and programmed in a code on the cracked microwave. A secret door sprang free beside him.

"You have got to be kidding me!" Molly exclaimed, eyes wide as she followed Julian into the darkness.

Devon motioned for Rae to follow and he glanced behind him to make sure no one was about. Satisfied, he followed her in. Molly's little electrical spark on her finger lit the passageway enough to take the blackness away. They moved silently, and once out of the small dark hallway they crouched, ready to react if Jennifer was there waiting for them.

Rae had to admit, she was impressed with Jennifer's hidden room and microwave connection.

But not nearly as impressed as she was when she emerged on the other side of the hallway.

Once they confirmed the coast was clear and Jennifer was nowhere to be found, Rae looked around. The apartment they were standing in now bore no resemblance to the one they'd just come from. In fact, it looked like it could have been on the cover of one of those interior design magazines. The rooms were bright and cheery, livened with tasteful splashes of color that matched the vibrant paintings on the walls. There were two suede sofas perched upon an expensive-looking Persian, a walk-in closet that made Molly's eyes water, and a plasma television that took up almost the entire wall upon which it was mounted.

"Throw pillows?" Rae murmured incredulously, picking one up to examine it. "Since when does Jennifer Jones like throw pillows?"

"Spread out," Devon commanded, ever the soldier. He ran through the rooms with Julian to confirm it was, in fact, empty. "Jenn's not here. Be sure to check everywhere: behind paintings, taped up beneath the bed, in the throw pillows, weaknesses on the floor. Everywhere." He turned to Rae and nodded seriously. "If those files are here, we're going to find them."

While Molly disappeared into the bathroom and the boys started prying up the floorboards in the foyer, Rae hurried down the hall to search the bedroom. Again, there was little inside that spoke to her of Jennifer. The comforter on the bed was a delicate shade of lilac, edged nicely between the sculpted frame, and there was a rocking chair in the corner draped with an actual quilt.

"What the hell?" she breathed, rubbing the edge of it between her fingers. Leave it to Devon to hear her.

"What's up, Rae?" he called a second later. "You find something?"

She dropped the quilt. "No, not yet."

Mentally kicking herself, she dropped her backpack in the middle of the floor and began the search. Now was no time to be asking herself existential questions about her ex-mentor. There may have been a time when the peculiarities of Jennifer Jones were of great interest to Rae, but that time ended about the time Jenn threw a car at her mom. Now, Rae was only concerned with finding her. Catching Jennifer, and finding the man who turned her against the PC agency and her friends in the first place.

And to do that, she needed to find those files.

If only wishing made it so.

The four of them searched the apartment for almost two hours—tearing the place apart as they wracked their brains for places to look. Molly found a hidden compartment of disguises and wigs, but no files. The boys stumbled on a lethal-looking weapons collection, which Rae helped herself to a few things. However, the files remained elusive.

Rae found something herself. But it wasn't something she was planning to share with the rest of the group.

She had stumbled into it by accident—literally tripping and throwing out her hands to steady herself as she ransacked a linen closet. When she knocked aside the balsa wood lining, she'd spotted the corner of a small wooden chest. Frowning to herself, she tugged it free and laid it on the floor to examine it more closely. It was the size of a small ottoman and was designed to look almost like some sort of toy chest. Rae's heart skipped a beat as she broke the lock between her fingers and pried open the lid.

What she saw stopped her dead in her tracks.

It wasn't the files she'd been hoping for.

It was baby clothes. A chest full of unused baby clothes. Most of the tags were still attached.

Rae put the chest back in the closet and shut the door without a word. The entire apartment, everything in it, suddenly made sense. This had been where Jennifer was hoping to raise her baby.

A delayed chill ran through Rae's shoulders and she walked slowly back to the kitchen to join the others. She didn't like to think of her little half-sister, killed by Simon Kerrigan before she had a chance to take her first breath. Rae knew that Jennifer had wanted to keep the baby, but her father had refused—insisting on a son. She wondered what things would have been like if the baby had been allowed to live. She'd have been starting Guilder about now. Who knows—maybe in Rae's own mentoring class. Would Rae have spent the entire year talking to this girl, teaching her to develop her powers, without ever knowing they were sisters?

The sight of her three friends snapped Rae from her reverie as she joined them. "Nothing?" she guessed at the disappointed looks on their faces.

Devon shook his head. "I just can't think of where else they'd be. This was Jenn's *place*. Her home base, you know?"

"Maybe she had another one," Molly volunteered. "After all, you guys knew about this place, so maybe she didn't think it was safe to—"

"But she was in London," Rae cut her off. "At the hospital and the hotel right across the street. She just wouldn't have had time to leave the city and stash them anywhere else—not when the freaking President of the Privy Council was with her all the time."

"You know," Devon turned to Julian, "now would be a great time to whip out one of those famous drawings of yours."

Julian sighed. "You know it doesn't work like that. Until one of us decides to open up the magic box where those files are hiding, I can't see it happening."

Molly frowned and stared around the kitchen.

"What about you Rae?" Julian asked. "You have a tatù that can find the bloody files?"

Rae shook her head and sighed. "We can't just go back empty-handed. What are we missing?" She was bordering on desperation. Without the files, they had no way of figuring out what Cromfield had been up to all this time. An already cold trail was starting to look a whole lot colder. More like frozen.

Molly silently backed away as Devon took a step forward to comfort her.

"We're not going back empty-handed." He raised her hands up to his lips and kissed them on the knuckles. "We're just going to have to figure out a different game plan if we want to—"

A loud bang made them jump. They whirled around to see Molly standing triumphantly by the open oven, a stack of files clenched in her hand.

"What the hell?" Julian scratched his head.

"It should have been obvious!" Molly grinned. "Like Jennifer would ever cook!" She shrugged. "I wouldn't cook. The stove looked brand new so I figured she might be like me and hide them in the most obvious spot so anyone would miss it. Except me, of course."

Rae jumped up on the balls of her feet and clapped her hands together. "Molls, you're a genius!" She held out her backpack and her best friend slipped the files casually inside.

"Of course I am. But before we get these back to the lab, I'm voting for a lunch break." She swept up her hair with a self-righteous sigh. "There's only so much a girl can do without caffeine. Or calories."

"I can't believe we're back at this bar." Rae shook her head incredulously, her backpack neatly tucked between her and Molly for safekeeping. She had pulled out a couple of files and scanned over them. Expecting to find secrets too dark for the Privy Council to even believe, she couldn't believe what were on the papers.

Nothing.

Well, barely nothing. Just missions the PC had done. Who had run them, what had been done, if it had been successful and if not, what repercussions had happened. The three Rae had grabbed from her bag were ones her mother had done. The PC probably had these same files on computer. They didn't seem like much help.

"There isn't much to go on here," Rae said, trying not to sound too disappointed. They'd come all this way for this?

Devon leaned over and looked at one of the files. "Maybe Jenn had gone off her rocker. Maybe she thought these were important."

"Or she was fascinated by your mother," Julian suggested. "And was trying to mimic your mother. Ironic that's the kind of tatù you have."

Rae closed the files and shoved them back in her bag. "Whatever they are, we'll have to go through them later. Right now, it's more important we find Jenn and Cromfield."

The four of them were sitting in a booth at the Second Sister—the ambiguously named pub where Carter and Jennifer had caught Devon, Molly, and Rae breaking curfew just a few days before. Four chocolate milkshakes lay before them, as well as four cappuccinos and four burgers with chips.

"What can I say?" Molly shrugged as she bit into her burger and spoke between chewing, "I got hooked on this coffee the last time I was here." She obviously felt the need to change the subject from the files that didn't seem very useful.

"I remember," Devon said with a strained smile, "I paid the bill."

She giggled into her milkshake. "You better get used to it, Devon. You're going to have to take Rae somewhere a lot nicer than this for graduation, and dates, and anniversaries, and your wedding."

Everyone looked up and away from each other at the same time. It seemed daring and beyond crazy to admit they were dating, but marriage? That thought wasn't even conceivable.

Rae quickly focused the conversation on another part of what Molly had said. "Wait. For graduation? What do you mean?"

The boys flashed each other a glance as Molly patted her hand consolingly. "Sometimes I forget how totally clueless you were when you first got to school. Of course, you wouldn't know. Every year, the Guilder graduates get this huge celebration party thrown in their honor. There's food, dancing, sometimes awards are even handed out for special achievements. The guest list is stacked—old alumni, members of the Privy Council. But, of course, each graduate is allowed to bring a date of their choosing."

Rae absorbed this for a moment before turning to Devon with a curious smile. "Who did you bring?" She pictured Devon's old girlfriend dressed stunningly beautiful.

He flashed his dimples. "She asks so casually..." The table laughed. "As much as I hate to disappoint you if you were looking for a juicy answer, I brought my grandmother. She was the one who passed the tatù to my father so she already knew all about them. Plus...she'd never been allowed inside Guilder because she was a woman. I thought she deserved a chance to see it."

Molly rolled her eyes and grinned, but Rae was truly smitten. Of course he brought his grandmother. Because everything from his toes up to those sexy dimples was absolutely perfect. It was also interesting to note his grandmother had the tatù. She was willing to bet Devon's father wasn't proud of that fact. "Well," she said, feigning disinterest, "if you're not doing anything else that night...maybe you'd like to go with me?"

His eyes sparkled. "Why Miss Kerrigan, are you asking me out on a date?"

Rae flicked a few drops of her milkshake at him. "Don't make me ask twice, Wardell," she teased. "If I have to ask again, the next guy I'm asking is Julian."

Julian chuckled. "No can do, darlin'. I'm going to be out of town."

"Out on another secret mission?" Molly asked. "Or out with the secret girl on a different kind of mission?" She raised her eyebrows up and down, trying to waggle them at Julian.

He raised his hand for the waitress. "Cheque, please."

Devon ignored them, keeping his eyes locked on Rae. "I'd love to go with you. I wish I'd had the courage last year to ask you."

Rae's stomach fluttered with automatic excitement, but she flashed a cool grin. "Well, okay then. I mean...if you insist."

He chuckled and pulled her in for a quick kiss.

But as they were packing up and heading back out to the car, Rae couldn't help but notice a small worried crease in the center of his forehead. When he saw her looking, he flashed a quick smile and hopped into the Jaguar, but Rae couldn't help but wonder.

Was this thing with his dad turning into an even bigger mess than she'd feared...?

They got back to Guilder just as the sun was setting through the tall trees. Groups of students were flooding out from the dining hall, and much to Rae's surprise, she found that she already recognized some faces. A few of the younger students even waved to her as the boys escorted her and Molly back to their rooms. Conscious of what she carried in her backpack, Rae pulled on the straps, keeping it close to her.

"So, we have the files...our first and only lead on Cromfield," Julian summarized as they trudged up the stairs. "Now we just need to find her."

Jennifer. The missing link.

Rae had gone over the problem a million times in her head. What it all came down to, was they were just stretched too thin. It was going to take everything she and her friends had just to pass their finals and graduate—not to mention searching for Cromfield both on their own and with their impromptu mentor group at the same time. Not only could she and Molly not get away from school and join the boys on the hunt, but Rae was extremely hesitant to leave her mom at a time like this.

Plus, there was one other major problem. Jennifer was a badass. There was a reason the PC had her teach Rae—she was one of the best fighters the Privy Council had ever employed. Or had Jennifer offered to teach Rae so she could get close to Rae?

It didn't matter. It was going to take a real force to bring her down. They needed someone as crazy and dangerous as Jennifer. Someone with nothing to lose.

Fortunately, Rae had someone in mind. "I think I know what's going to help us," she said tentatively, suddenly dodging their curious looks.

"What do you mean?" Devon asked.

"I know someone that can help us."

She'd sent the text late last night after dinner. It was the very definition of a long shot, but at this point, she figured it was the only shot they had.

"Who?" Devon asked curiously.

Just then they arrived at Rae's door. A dead black rose had been nailed to the front of it.

"Perfect!" Rae forced a smile and tried to sound cheerful. "He got my message."

Chapter 6

"You have *got* to be kidding me!"

Devon's handsome face turned an angry shade of puce. They'd moved inside her room when she'd told them what she had done. Rae seriously worried that if he didn't calm down, he might burst a major artery, or hyperventilate or something that would require medical attention. She wanted to go through the files but now was obviously not the time to suggest it.

She held up her hands peaceably. "Honey, think about it. It's not that bad of an idea—"

"Don't you *honey* me! There's absolutely no way we're getting Kraigan involved in this! The guy tried to *kill* you, Rae—half a dozen times!"

Rae glanced at Molly and Julian for help, but they were suddenly keeping their eyes wisely on the ground. *All right Kerrigan*, she told herself. *You expected some resistance. You just have to stand your ground.* "Okay, but for one thing—he didn't try to kill me *that* many times."

Devon flashed her a look of sheer consternation and even Molly glanced up with a frown.

All right—bad strategy. Moving on.

"For another thing—Kraigan doesn't have any sort of motive to kill me anymore. Hate me, sure, but not kill me." She said the words in a rush, trying to get them all out before Devon stopped her. "He thought I was some golden child, the one whose mother was chosen and that's why his own mother got killed. But we know now that's not the case. My family had nothing to do with his mother's death—it was all Jennifer."

Julian started nodding slowly and Devon swatted him upside the head.

Rae continued cautiously, taking a slight step back just to make sure she was out of back-of-the-head range. "No one in the world has a greater motivation to catch Jennifer than he does. AND no one stands a better chance at doing exactly that. He's intelligent, devious, and dangerous."

Devon flashed a pained expression and she steered clear of the 'lethal' words.

Rae crossed her arms over her chest, she refused to be deterred from her decision. "I mean—he's *capable*. If anyone can catch her, it's him. Plus, once he does, he simply has to absorb her power and she'll be defenseless." Rae smiled at the idea. "Like a cat without claws."

Devon was obviously waiting on pins and needles until she finished her speech. Now that she was done talking, he crossed the room and stood right in front of her, forcing her to look in his eyes. "Rae, that's all well and good, except that Kraigan isn't known to be the most rational kind of guy. He flat-out worshiped your father, and in his twisted mind, that alone was enough reason to come after you."

"But that's the thing," Rae said quickly. "Once he knows how Simon treated his mother—like some animal to be used for breeding—he'll hate him, and Jennifer, just as much as I do."

"Rae, you can't—"

"Trust me, Devon." She looked deep into his troubled eyes. "Jennifer killed his mom. If there's one thing he'll care about more than hating me, it's that."

Molly's voice ventured tentatively from the corner. "How in the world are you going to convince him that's the case? He thinks the entire thing is on you and your mom. He's not going to believe you if you just call him up one day and tell him that's not true anymore."

The corners of Rae's lips turned up in a little smile. "Of course he won't. That's why I have to *show* him."

A brief silence followed her proclamation. Followed by an explosion.

"You WHAT?!"

"Rae, come on, you can't be serious—"

"Even I can't go along with you on that one..."

She held up her hands for silence. When that didn't work, she covered those hands in fire. The boys fell suddenly quiet and Molly folded her arms angrily over her chest.

"You know I don't like it when you do that inside," she accused. "It makes all my clothes smell like smoke! Even from across the hall."

Rae doused the flames at once and forced herself to calmly face her friends. "Guys, I don't like getting that close to him any more than you do. *However*, it's our best shot, and you know it. It might be our only shot."

Julian stared at the floor and Molly frowned out the window, but Devon was still looking at Rae with cold steel in his eyes. This was a course of action he simply couldn't sanction.

Rae tried again. "All I need to do is let him touch me for a split second. He'll absorb Carter's gift and be able to see everything I saw for myself. When he catches Jennifer—and we all know he will catch her eventually—he can use the same thing on her."

Still, her friends said nothing. She looked at each one of them desperately in turn, until finally landing on her reluctant boyfriend. "Devon, please. You know it's a good idea."

He regarded her for a moment, but slowly shook his head. "No, I can't help you seek out the man who tried to end your life. I won't do it."

A rush of emotion swelled in her chest, but she tried to keep herself under control. "This isn't about me—this is about Cromfield! He killed my father, brainwashed my mother, and left me to grow up as an orphan. And he's still out there! Devon...please! It's a risk worth taking." She pulled herself up to her full height. "And I'm taking it."

Devon studied her for a long moment, clenching his jaw so hard she thought it might break, before suddenly crossing to her desk. He ripped off a sheet of binder paper and grabbed a pencil, and then thrust them both in Julian's face. Julian took them tentatively, staring back and forth between Rae and Devon with a question in his eye.

"Draw," Devon commanded. "Draw what happens if we go and meet Kraigan."

With a silent nod, Julian perched on the edge of the mattress. His eyes grew unfocused for a moment, before glassing over as his hand began flying over the page. Despite the charged atmosphere in the room, Rae couldn't help but take an inquisitive step closer. She'd seen Julian draw before, but it was nothing like this. His eyes were almost completely opaque as his hand swept over the page; connecting lines and shading angles that made no sense to anyone but him.

Devon saw her watching and followed her gaze. "It's been like this for a while now," he explained. "One day, he just seemed different than before. The drawings are more detailed, complex. They even depict things happening further and further down the road."

"Can he hear us?" Rae asked curiously.

Devon walked over to Julian and gently kicked his foot. He waved a hand once or twice in front of his face, but there was no response, no sound except the hasty scratches of the pencil. "He's completely out of it. It's like he goes into some sort of trance. It's been like this since... since..."

"Since he started drawing me?" Rae asked.

Devon could only shrug a maybe yes.

Molly raised her eyebrows. "Well, that's useful. I mean, if it enhances his visions."

Devon nodded, but watched his friend with a worried crease. "As long as he only gets the visions at an appropriate time. He's completely defenseless when it happens. It leaves him vulnerable."

Just then, Julian's eyes cleared back to their deep brown and he stared unblinkingly around the room, like a man who'd just woken up from a sudden sleep.

"Welcome back, buddy," Devon smiled quickly, then gestured to the paper. "So, how about it? What's it going to be?"

Julian frowned and stared down at his drawing. "I only drew him touching her. I can't tell what happens next because he hasn't decided it himself."

He held up the paper and Rae had to stop herself from gasping aloud at the perfection of the portrait. It was like he'd simply taken a photograph and shaded it in black and white. Each minute detail was colored with a flawless hand, lending an almost eerie sense of foreboding to the little scene. A sense that was increased tenfold when she saw that Kraigan had his hands around her neck.

"Well, that doesn't look very good," Molly murmured.

"See!" Devon declared. "He's trying to kill you. We're not going."

Rae countered fiercely. "*Or* he's taking Carter's tatù like I want him to."

"With his hands around your neck?!"

Julian muttered, "You have to admit, it's Kraigan's style."

"Thank you, Julian!" Rae stared at Devon in triumph.

Julian's face paled, making it almost white in the moonlight. "I'm not saying I think you should go."

"Aha!" Devon countered, pointing to his friend with a grin.

Julian held up his hands and backed away. "Look, I'm not getting in the middle of this. But guys, you have to keep in mind that this isn't some kind of lover's quarrel, all right? This is a mission, just like any other. Please at least try to be pragmatic."

Devon turned on him. "Pragmatic? That's a bit hypocritical, don't you think? If this were you and me dealing with any other agent we'd ever worked with, we'd be out the door already. But you don't want to go either because it's Rae."

Julian met his friend's anger with gentle patience. "Rae can take care of herself."

"Yeah, she can," Molly interjected suddenly. "And we'll all be there with her."

Devon stared at the other two like they'd literally stabbed him in the back. "You guys cannot be seriously considering this."

"It's three against one, Devon," Rae said softly, putting her hand on his arm. "We're going."

Devon ripped the arm away and took her by the shoulders, pulling her forward so their faces were only inches apart. "You can't ask me to do this," he begged quietly. "It's like every other day I have to stand by and watch as someone new tries to kill you, Rae. I get that, it's part of dating Rae Kerrigan. But let's at least not go willingly back to someone who's already tried it before. *Please.*"

Rae stroked the side of his face with a tender look in her eye. "I hate to say it, but that's also part of dating a Kerrigan. In case you didn't pick it up from the family dinner last night, or even just by getting to know me these last few years, we've got a bit of a wild streak."

His lips curled up into a smile in spite of himself, and the next thing she knew, they were kissing. For the first time, she didn't care that her two friends were in the room watching. She threw her arms around his neck and kissed him with reckless abandon, only pulling away when Molly cleared her throat sharply from across the room.

"Do *not* make me throw up my milkshake. I forbid it."

Julian turned away to the window with a grin. "So much for keeping things professional."

Devon grinned but it quickly disappeared. He held Rae close as she pulled out her phone to text Kraigan back.

"I'm telling him to meet us back at that pub in London." Her fingers flew over the keys on her phone. She was glad nobody asked how she had gotten his text number. She herself had it from when he had been in Guilder pretending to be someone else, but couldn't be sure he'd kept his phone. The rose on the door had proven he'd read the message.

"Have him meet us there at midnight," Devon instructed. "That gives us time to get there an hour or two before to scope it out for any little surprises he might have up his sleeve."

Rae typed it into her phone, then slipped it back in her pocket. "Done." She fought back the automatic shudder, which ran through her skin at the thought of seeing her half-brother again. Last time he'd tried to burn her at the old Wade factory. Speaking of which, she glanced at the figurines in the small cabinet on her desk. She'd have to ask her mother if she remembered them also. There was still the message to decode. She'd done some of it, but was pretty sure there was more to the whole thing. Now was not the time to think about that though. Pushing the thoughts of her mother aside, she stuffed her backpack in the back of her closet and slipped on her coat. "No one's going to look for the files here." She shrugged. "No one knows we have them."

"Yet," Molly added with a yawn. "I think we should start keeping stuff in my room. No one ever sneaks into my room." She looked purposely at Devon.

"Shall we get going then?" Devon asked and turned to reach for the doorknob.

Rae laughed as she went through the door Devon held open for her.

The boys and Molly followed suit and headed out behind her down the stairs. Halfway down, Devon grabbed Julian's keys with a wry smile. "How 'bout I drive?"

A look of sheer frustration clouded Julian's face. "I'll be *fine*," he muttered.

"I know you would," Devon answered just as softly. "But let's just leave this to me for now, okay pal? Precious cargo and all..."

The entire exchange was lost on Molly, who stepped in front of Rae on the stairs when Rae slowed her gait down to listen to the boys. Rae switched into an advanced hearing tatù and followed along curiously. If they were planning to take Julian's car, it would seem natural Julian would drive. Although, come to think of it, he hadn't been driving earlier today in London either, and he'd complained when she had zapped Devon on the shoulder while he was driving. Was something the matter with him? Had he lost his license? Worse, was he sick?

Before Rae had a chance to ask, she walked headlong into the back of Molly and almost fell down the rest of the stairs. Luckily Molly stood solid to keep them from tumbling. The boys, in turn, ran into her, and all of them lifted their heads together to see why Molly had stopped so suddenly.

Madame Elpis stood tapping her foot near the front door of Aumbry House. Her wiry arms folded tightly across her body and her beady eyes locking on each one of their guilty faces in turn.

Devon was the first to recover. "Hey, Madame Elpis. Lovely night..."

She gave him a look so sharp it could cut through glass. "*Night* being the operative word, Mr. Wardell. Where exactly do you and the rest of your friends think you're going at this hour?"

Devon swallowed hard and fell back into the group. Technically speaking, he and Julian didn't attend the school, and thus didn't fall under the school curfew rules. But there was something about Madame Elpis that made you feel as though anything and everyone were under her jurisdiction. All the time.

Molly flashed her a sweet smile. "We were just going out for a little walk to clear our heads. We've been studying so much for finals I think mine might fall right off..." Her voice petered out as she stared at the strict headmistress of Aumbry House.

"Both you and Miss Kerrigan are still under curfew," she answered sharply. "There's no wandering the grounds after nine p.m. and you know it. Now get back to your rooms."

Rae cleared her throat and tried to sound braver than she was. "Actually, the curfew for seniors is eleven p.m. I believe..." She let her words trail off when Madame Elpis harrumphed. Rae decided to try a different route. "The four of us have business for the Privy Council and we—"

"Both you and Mr. Wardell were suspended from the Privy Council," Elpis cut her off. "The headmaster made sure the faculty were all informed. It's come to my attention that both Miss Skye and—" Her head turned sharply as Julian moved a step back up the stairs. "You too, *Julian*, are on a temporary leave of absence, so allow me to repeat myself." She put her hands on her hips and all four teenagers fell back another step. "Go back to your rooms."

In a flurry of hasty nods and averted eye contact, Rae and the others tripped all over themselves to head back to her dorm room. As they high-tailed it back up the stairs, they heard Elpis call out behind them, "You're lucky that seniors are allowed co-ed study groups or you gentlemen would be banished back to your side of campus!"

"She's so interfering," Molly complained as she slammed Rae's door on the top story in a huff. "I really think we need to do some sort of love intervention—find her a man. Wasn't she dating Professor What's His Name's brother? Donald something?" She threw her hands up in frustration. "That obviously didn't work out. She needs a man! It's the only way she's ever going to develop some basic human traits. You know...like compassion."

"Fat chance," Devon grinned as he helped Rae push open the window. "Could you imagine dating her? She's terrifying." He caught Rae's eye and flushed self-consciously. "I mean, she doesn't terrify *me*, but...other people...maybe."

Rae laughed and leaned against the open frame as her boyfriend threw himself carelessly out the three-story drop, landing lightly on his feet. Rae followed right behind him and Julian next. Molly took a bit of convincing but Devon and Julian caught her easily. They stomped happily over the grass out to the parking lot.

Only to run into Madame Elpis. Again.

Rae's heart leapt to her throat and Molly made a strange little squeaking sound as they froze in their tracks once more. This time, not a word was said. The four of them just took one look at her and spun around in their tracks, heading back to the dormitory in silence.

"Well, we'll just have to wait it out here for an hour or so until Julian sees that she's gone to bed. Or we sneak past her room when she's snoring," Devon muttered as they settled back down in Rae's room.

"And until then?" Rae looked around the room, her eyes settling on the closet. Maybe they could go through the files.

"Until then, we get some sleep while we can," Julian answered, settling into a chair with a sweater scrunched up beneath him as a pillow. "Looks like it's going to be another all-nighter."

"It seems like that's all we've been having lately," Molly whined as she climbed onto the chair beside him and cuddled in beneath his arm. "Don't bad guys know," she yawned loudly, "that we need to sleep?"

"Dev?" Julian asked routinely as he hitched Molly higher on his lap and shut his eyes.

"Yeah," Devon replied automatically. "I'll wake you in an hour to see if the coast is clear from ol' hawk eyes."

He pointed to the bed. He and Rae curled up together on top of the sheets and watched as their two friends succumbed quickly to sleep. It wasn't long before Molly and Julian's breathing had shallowed and steadied out, leaving their faces relaxed and peaceful.

"They both look so much younger when they sleep," Rae whispered with a grin, staring at her two friends.

The juxtaposition was hilarious. Julian was all long and lean with his tanned skin, sleek dark hair, and legs that seemed to stretch all the way to the door. Molly was a different thing entirely. All curled up, she probably only took up about a third of his body, and her vibrant crimson hair splayed out across his chest made it seem as though he'd suffered a recent knife wound. When contrasted to his, her fair skin was shockingly pale, and every now and then, little sparks would flick from the tips of her fingers. He would flinch each time they hit him, but his arm would tighten automatically—even in sleep—to keep her supported on the chair.

"So do you," Devon whispered back with a grin. His lips brushed against her hair.

Rae could feel his warm breath against her scalp. It sent a shiver down her back. The good kind. She turned to him in surprise. "You've watched me sleep?" She tried to sound accusing even though she couldn't help but smile. She most certainly had done the same thing to him.

"Oh no," his face tightened in a mock frown, "I would never."

He opened his arm and she slid inside without a second thought, nestling up against his side as she stared out the window. For as much as she'd advocated this particular plan, she had to admit, the idea of seeing Kraigan again terrified her. You couldn't be trapped in an underground lair with a guy pouncing on top of you and draining all your powers without that happening.

But Kraigan would see the truth she told herself again and again. He would see that none of this was her fault. Sure, they'd never be friends, let alone the family that they technically were, but he shouldn't have any further reason to want her dead.

She rolled over so her back was spooning Devon's chest. She stifled a little sigh. *Shouldn't* didn't exactly mean *wouldn't* in Kraigan's book. As incredible as Julian's drawing had been, she wished he'd been able to see just a little bit more.

She turned her neck so she could look at Devon. "What was that about earlier, on the stairs with Julian? Why won't you let him drive?"

For a moment, Devon looked uncomfortable. He glanced over at his friend, but it was clear Julian was fast asleep. After a moment of watching, he sighed. "Julian and I were in Spain a couple of weeks ago—on a mission for the PC. We were speeding down this country road in a rental, when all of a sudden, Julian got a vision. It was stronger than anything he'd ever had before—like the one you saw today—and it came out of the blue. No warning or anything." He shifted almost nervously and bit his lip. "Unfortunately, Julian was the one driving the car."

Rae's jaw dropped open. "What happened?!"

"The car flipped, sent me flying through the windshield. Julian didn't even feel it—he was in a trance. It's probably the reason why he wasn't really hurt, his body was completely relaxed."

"But you went through the windshield?!" Rae demanded in a fierce whisper.

Devon stroked back her hair soothingly. "Rae, it wasn't his fault. And trust me, when he came to, he felt horrible. There was no predicting—"

"I'm not saying it was his fault." She pulled herself into a sitting position. "I'm saying, you were in a car accident in Spain and you didn't even tell me. Devon, what if something happens to you in some remote corner of the globe and I don't hear about it until weeks later, if I hear about it at all?"

"That's not going to happen," he assured her, kissing her on the forehead. "In fact, there's even less of a personal risk now that our powers are developing so quickly. We just need to get through a couple of speed bumps along the way." He flashed her a quirky grin.

"Speed bumps?" she repeated in disbelief.

"Too soon?"

She chuckled softly and smacked him on the arm before settling back against his chest. "So, that's why you're not letting Julian drive?"

Devon nodded. "At first, he was completely on board. But his visions haven't caught him unawares for almost two months now and he's getting restless." Rae felt him shrug behind her. "I can understand. It has to feel a little claustrophobic—almost like they're holding him captive, controlling him instead of the other way around."

Rae mulled this over as she pulled his arms tight around her. She could certainly sympathize with the feeling herself. When she'd gotten her first flood of new powers, she was almost afraid to be in the same room as the people she cared about. She never knew which one was going to come flooding to the surface and catch her off guard. And as strong as each of her tatùs were, none of them, except the ones given to her by her parents, had come close to matching Julian's in terms of development. It was actually kind of thrilling to know that each one had the capacity for so much growth. Who knew where she'd be in just a year or two's time?

In the same breath, she echoed some of Devon's worry. Now was not the time for anyone on her team to be even remotely vulnerable. Not when they'd be seeing Kraigan in just a few short hours. Who knew what the psycho had up his sleeve? She stifled another shudder.

She couldn't stand it if Devon was right about Kraigan.

Just as long as he didn't actually try to *kill* her again.

Chapter 7

"I don't care, okay? I'm sure there's a better way to go about it."

"What's wrong, man? You don't like falling into my arms?" Devon grinned mischievously and Julian shot him a withering glare.

"I'm just saying, if we're going to be jumping out of Rae's third-story window on a regular basis, maybe we should invest in a rope ladder or something. Not all of us have your guys' weird little fox power..."

"Okay, first off; it's not *our* power, it's *my* power. My darling girlfriend just steals it from time to time."

"Mimics it," Rae interjected from the back seat.

The boys ignored her.

"And second; I seem to remember my 'weird little fox power' saving your ass on more than one occasion, so you might want to show some respect."

A hundred streetlamps flew past as they raced down the darkened interstate, staining everyone's faces with an intermittent orange glow.

Julian cocked his head. "Wait a minute...I'm having a vision here. Oh yeah! It's of me punching you in the nose. That's odd, isn't it?"

Devon flashed a devilish grin. "You might want to hold off on that for now seeing as *I'm the one who's driving...*"

Julian opened his mouth to say something else, but Rae held up her hands. "Enough! We're all going to need to focus if we're about to meet Kraigan."

"Which I still think is a bad idea."

Molly kicked the back of Devon's chair, but Rae just smiled sweetly. "Yes, honey, you've made that abundantly clear."

He glanced back in the rearview mirror, and for a moment, Rae forgot her teasing and the mission and stared, simply entranced. It was impossible not to be. Flying down the highway with stars and flashes of light streaking by, Devon's dark eyes seemed depthless. Deep chestnut pools with no end in sight. How could one *not* lose themselves in those eyes? *Sigh.*

Suddenly, his brow creased in a question and she realized she had been staring a bit too long. At the same time, Julian groaned softly from the front seat.

"What is it?" Molly asked with concern.

"I just saw the two of them kissing the second we get out of the car." He rubbed his temples like the entire ordeal had been very trying for him. "This is getting ridiculous. It's getting *constant*, now. I can't just close my eyes anymore without seeing things. Rae seems to be in the hot seat, starring as the main character. Just like the drawings."

The drawings had been left on a shelf in her brain to ask about another day. Now was not the day. Rae put her hands on his shoulders. "Visions? Or Devon and I kissing?"

Julian's lips twitched up in a reluctant smile. "Both. Equally terrible."

"Well, why don't you do something useful with your gift and scan ahead for cops?" Devon pulled off at an exit. "We're coming into the city."

For a second, Julian's dark eyes turned pearl in the moonlight. Then he brought himself out of it and shook his head. "No one's going to pull us over. Drive as fast as you want."

Devon put his foot to the floor and the car lurched forward as they raced down a shadowy side street away from the main roads. Rae could almost feel the tension growing more and more palpable the closer they got to the Second Sister, and by the time the pub was within sight, all four of them were glued to the windows.

Devon circled around once, searching for anything out of the ordinary, before pulling into the back of the parking lot. The friends paused for a moment, safe from sight behind the tinted windows, before both boys turned around in unison for a last-minute huddle.

"Okay, so we just stick to the plan," Devon said, and then dropping his voice so only Rae could hear, "There's no telling what kind of tatù Kraigan is currently working with." He cleared his throat and continued, "Molls, you stun him. Julian, come around behind. I'll attack from the front. And Rae—"

"Yeah, I know." Her three friends watched in wonder as she melted away into thin air. "I'm invisible."

"That's so freakin' creepy..." Molly whispered.

"Cool," Julian corrected.

Devon didn't smile or acknowledge their comments. He was all business. "Let's go." He lowered his voice again to a whisper only another tatù like his could hear. "Remember to go out Molly's door and let her close it."

The other two started piling out of the car, as Rae slipped back into sight, if only for a moment, and grabbed Devon's sleeve. "Aren't you forgetting something?"

He looked at her blankly for a moment. "No, what?"

She pulled them together with no warning, kissing him long and hard even as she faded back out of sight. When Devon opened his eyes again, there was nothing but air.

"Julian saw us kiss," she whispered.

He grinned automatically, then swiped blindly at the air, knocking her shoulder.

"Ouch," she giggled under her breath, "nice follow through."

"Sorry," he chuckled, "that's going to take a little getting used to." He straightened back up and held upon his door. "You ready?"

"Let's do this."

Without another word, Molly, Julian, and Devon made their way slowly across the parking lot to the pub. Rae followed along a few steps behind, marveling at how even her shadow was invisible, taking care not to step in any puddles. It wasn't until they were about halfway across that everything seemed to go suddenly wrong.

"Wait a minute," Julian murmured, putting his hand to his temple. The next second, his eyes glassed over and he fell to his knees, overwhelmed with the strength of the vision.

Devon was by his side in a moment. "Julian!" He tried to help him up, but his friend wouldn't budge. "Snap out of it, man! What is it? What do you see?"

A loud *click* echoed across the empty lot. A sound each of them knew instinctively. A sound none of them could ever forget.

All the hair on the back of Rae's neck stood on end as she looked up in horror.

It was Kraigan, all right. Holding a gun.

"Well, good evening!" he said overly cheerful. "Or should I say good morning? You cut it so close, we might have passed midnight already."

Molly raised her fingers a fraction of an inch and he pointed the gun directly at her heart.

"Aw Molls," Kraigan kept smiling, but there was something chilling buried just beneath the surface, "you wouldn't want to do anything *stupid*, would you?"

In a flash, Devon left Julian on the pavement and launched himself at Kraigan, keeping his body in between the gun and Molly. He moved so fast he was nothing but a rush of air and a blur of colors. Rae didn't need Julian's gift to know what Kraigan was going to do next.

Just as Devon knocked the gun into the air, Kraigan whipped around and grabbed the bare skin on the side of his neck. He needed only a moment for his ink to take effect. Devon's eyes grew wide and disoriented, and the next second, he stumbled back across the wet concrete, staring around him in horror as he tried to stand.

Rae knew firsthand what it felt like to have one's tatù taken away. It was like losing an arm or a leg—something as fundamental as breathing. There was no greater violation.

"Wow," Kraigan closed his eyes as he savored the sensation, "I missed this one."

"You bastard." Devon's whole body was twitching, stripped of its usual sensitivity. "I swear, if you touch them I'll—"

Then Devon was on the ground. Rae had to stifle a shriek as he skidded to her feet, bleeding from a cut beneath his eye.

"Shit!" Kraigan chuckled, rubbing his knuckles. "Yeah, your tatù lets you hit that hard, but it sure doesn't dull the pain when you do, does it? And as for the other thing..." He shot forward and kicked Devon in the ribs before he had a chance to stand. "I think you're hardly in a position to be making threats."

With an enraged cry, Molly fired a wide band of crackling lightening, but Kraigan both ducked and recovered the gun before it could do any harm. He straightened with a sinister laugh, pointing it once more at her chest. "Try it again, I dare you." His eyes glared dangerously. Having their full attention, he straightened, keeping the gun trained on Molly and ready to pounce on Devon. "Let's see...the Privy Council sends out their best and brightest and look what happens. One is held hostage to his own ink, another loses his tatù altogether, and the only one still standing is the little fashionista." He clucked his tongue disapprovingly. "Hardly a worthwhile fight. And I have to say, not the fight I was expecting." He took a few steps forward, lifting the gun to Molly's head. "Tell me Miss Skye...where is my bitch of a sister?"

"*Right behind you.*"

Rae sank her teeth into Kraigan's hand hard enough to draw blood, and again, the gun went flying across the parking lot. He cursed and whirled around, but she used Jennifer's speed, leaping out of reach and crushing the pistol to a pulp before he could touch her.

As she dusted the metal from her hands, she regarded him with a smile. "Hello there, *dear* brother."

Instead of lunging at her as she expected, Kraigan burst into slow applause. Each clap echoed in the tiny lot and sent a shiver up her spine, but she stood tall. She could not let him unnerve her. She knew what she had to do.

"Well done, sis. Well done." He grinned and walked casually closer. "Using your friends as bait so you could sneak in for the kill? It's a good plan. A little heartless for you I would think, but still commendable." He clapped once more.

Her face tightened, but she forced herself to keep smiling. "Well, I didn't expect you to bring an actual gun. That's stooping pretty low. Who brings a gun to a tatù fight?" She shrugged one shoulder. "But I guess I should have seen that coming. Either way, I didn't come here to fight you, Kraigan."

He advanced a few more steps. "As much as I hate to disappoint you, that's exactly what you're going to—"

"I saw your mother die."

All the smiling foreplay vanished as he froze in place. "Trust me, Kerrigan," there was almost no color left around his eyes, "that's not a game you want to play with me."

He flew towards her, but she grabbed him by the sleeves and threw him into a truck, watching impassively as he slid to the ground.

"She was killed by a woman named Jennifer Jones. A rogue agent in the PC. A woman who was kind enough to give me this tatù I'm using to kick your ass. She was in love with our dad, and when he wouldn't leave either of our mothers to be with her, she set the fire. She was hoping to eliminate the comp—"

"That's not true!" Kraigan roared, pulling himself to his feet. "We both know *exactly* what you and your mother are. We know exactly whose fault this is!"

Rae stared him straight in the eyes. "Your mother showed up at the house when Simon and my mom were arguing. Jennifer was hiding upstairs. She lit the fire. It had nothing to do with us."

"SHUT UP!"

His face was paler than Rae had ever seen, making his dark curls shine against his skin. She took a deep breath. If they hadn't had such a violent history, she'd almost feel sorry for him. "The ceiling collapsed on your mother and our dad. They died instantly."

"That's impossible. It's not true—stop lying!" He rushed at her again, but she deflected him easily. His heart wasn't really in it.

"Give it up, Kraigan."

He stood again and wiped the blood from his lower lip. He hadn't taken her tatù, but he still had Devon's. "Why on earth do you think I'd believe you?"

This time, it was Rae who stepped forward. "I don't." She sighed. "I don't think you'd believe it unless you saw it with your own eyes."

"Damn right."

"I can show you." She held out her hands and he paused. "Let me show you."

His eyes flickered to where Molly and Devon were dragging Julian out of the street and into the back seat of the car before returning to Rae. "If this is some kind of trick—"

"No trick," she said calmly. "I have a tatù which allows me to go back in people's memories. I used it on Jennifer last week and I saw the whole thing. I can show you now."

He took a step forward but halted warily, like a kid reaching his hand out to a snake.

"What do you think I'm going to do, Kraigan?" she asked softly. "I never wanted to see you again. Why on earth would I text you if it wasn't the truth?"

There was a split second where he seemed to make up his mind, then he strode forward with confidence and wrapped his hands around her neck. Rae reached hers around his. "We'll see, won't we?" he growled. "And if you're lying, rest assured I'll just—"

His eyes snapped shut as the vision took hold. Rae focused. She tried to stay centered only on the memory of what she saw—not let other parts of her life seep in. At first there were flashes of her with her mom at dinner the other night...then a flash of her with Devon. Kraigan leaned forward with sudden interest, but Rae forced the memory back to the day at the hotel.

Kraigan's whole body stiffened as he watched. His eyes tensed at the image and he squeezed Rae's hand so hard she thought it might break. She followed along, watching as he watched, seeing the same things she'd seen before that day. It was deeply unsettling. To feel the wet pavement beneath her feet, but smell the acrid stench of burning plaster in the air. She focused on breathing, like she'd been taught a long time ago.

When they got to the part where the ceiling actually fell through, crushing the two people underneath, Kraigan made a half-strangled sound and jerked away, letting go of her neck. "Stop!" There were actual tears in his eyes as he started backing slowly away. "I can't see anymore. I can't—"

"You have to," Rae said firmly, grabbing his hand. "You need to know."

With a gasp, they were both pulled back into the vision. This time, things happened very quickly. It was clear that Simon and Kraigan's mother were dead. And it was clear from how Simon had treated her, that he hadn't cared for the woman one bit. Rae directed all her focus to the memory now, fixing their joined attention on the smoldering kitchen. She knew what was coming.

The smoke cleared, the plaster settled. Then there she was. Jennifer.

Rae allowed Kraigan to see just enough of the argument between Jennifer and Beth to ensure his immortal hatred before pulling her hand suddenly away. There was no point in showing him how Cromfield fit into the picture—they were having enough trouble with that as it was. They needed Kraigan to turn into a one-man wrecking ball with one specific target.

The look on his face when he opened his eyes told her she'd got what she wanted.

"Jennifer. Jones?" He said the name slowly, like he was trying it out.

Rae nodded silently. "She did the whole thing. She wanted revenge for Simon."

"And my mother," his voice tightened at the word, "was just there at the wrong time?"

There was such a vulnerable look on his frightening, murderous face that Rae had to remind herself who she was talking to. "Yes, I believe she was. I'm...I'm sorry, Kraigan. Had I known sooner, I'd have told you. That's why I got in contact with you." She cringed as his jaw clenched tight together. "You deserved to know."

Devon and Molly were standing on either side of her now. The second she'd touched Kraigan, Devon had his tatù back and from the way he was sporadically clenching and unclenching his fists, he was eager to return the beating he'd taken earlier. The sparks shooting from Molly's fingers were a pretty clear indicator she'd like to do the same.

When he saw them, Kraigan straightened and bravely cast them his cocky smile. It was almost believable. "So, what now, Rae? You want me to kill this woman?" He tutted. "That doesn't seem like the Rae Kerrigan way. Or the PC way."

Rae glanced down at the pavement. He couldn't think it was some kind of order or request, he'd never go along with it that way. But perhaps there was a different way she could phrase it. "This woman is supposed to be my mentor. She helped train me. Taught me everything she knew."

His face grew hard. "I knew it! You want me to spare her."

Rae looked him dead in the eye. "I'm saying, I won't stand in your way."

That was enough for Kraigan. Without another word, he strode off across the parking lot and into the night.

"Wait!" Rae ran after him, switching to a tatù with quickness. "Where are you going?"

He glanced behind, incredulous that she would follow him, but did not stop walking.

"I—We have information to help you. Kraigan, her tatù's crazy strong. No one's been able to find her so far—"

"I'll find her."

"But what if you need—"

He stopped so quickly she would have walked right into him if he hadn't caught her in his arms. For the first time all night, a hint of a genuine smile softened his features. It didn't last. He pushed her away like her touch burned his skin. "I said I'll find her. I know a friend with a nice little tracking tatù which should come in handy."

"Who?" She tried to think if it was someone she knew.

"Don't worry, sis, I know where to get one."

He started walking away again and Rae threw up her hands. "Well...good luck, I guess."

"And for the record," he called over his shoulder, "this doesn't make us even."

Rae's jaw dropped open. "*Excuse* me?! You're the one who's always trying to kill me!"

"Yeah, well," he flashed her a grin, "we've got a temporary truce." A second later, he vanished into the night.

Rae turned back to her friends, but they looked just as incredulous as she did. She realized he'd stolen her speed tatù. "Dickhead!" she mumbled under her breath.

Molly threw her hands in the air. "Well, if anyone's crazy enough to get into Jennifer's head, it's Kraigan," she said.

Devon shook his head, a dark hatred simmering in his eyes. "Temporary truce, my ass," he muttered.

Rae tried to smile. "Believe it or not, a temporary truce is great progress for Kraigan and me. Can we go home now? Before anything else can happen? I think I've had quite enough surprises tonight. How's Julian by the way? Have you guys been keeping an eye on him?"

Devon slapped his forehead and ran to the car, with Rae right on his heels. Julian still lay stretched out in the back of the car when they checked, his eyes glazed over with a glassy, milky haze.

"What's wrong with him," Rae murmured, scared he might not wake up. "Why hasn't he snapped out of it yet?"

Devon chewed his lower lip. "I don't know. It's never gone on this long before."

"Let's get him back," Molly said with determination. "Carter and the PC doctors at Guilder will be able to sort it out."

They piled into the car and shot away from London as fast as possible. Molly seemed still visibly shaken from having a gun pointed at her head, and Devon was no doubt sporting a few cracked ribs, which he tried valiantly to hide when he saw Rae was watching. Rae sat in the back with Julian, his head cradled in her lap.

It wasn't until they actually pulled onto the long Guilder drive that Julian sat up with a start.

"He's got a gun!" he shouted.

The other three jumped in alarm, then shot each other tired, worried looks.

"Yeah," Devon said and smirked. "Thanks, man."

"Wait a minute." Julian looked around. "Why're we back at school?"

"I'll fill you in later," Devon said in a clipped tone before swearing under his breath. "We've got company."

"Oh poppy-cock!" Molly mumbled from the front seat and pointed at the front window.

Madame Elpis stood in the parking lot with her arms folded across her chest, side by side with Dean Wardell.

Rae's stomach sank at the triumphant look across the Dean's face—a look that was only slightly dampened when he saw his son was also in the car.

She may have literally dodged a few bullets tonight, but one thing was certain.

Rae had detention.

Chapter 8

There was nothing more insulting than sitting in detention because you got caught coming back from a virtual suicide mission trying to save the world.

Not *the* world, of course. But the world of tatùs. A community of people that Rae was beginning to suspect were increasingly ungrateful for all her efforts.

That, and she couldn't tell the Dean or Madame Elpis what they had just gone and done. PC secret. Bull crap!

She stretched her arms out across the desk and examined her fingernails with an inaudible sigh. Sitting two chairs away, Molly fired sparks absentmindedly from one hand to the other, her eyes glassed over with boredom as she stared fixedly at nothing.

When Dean Wardell had caught them—more specifically, *Rae*—off school grounds after curfew, Rae had thought his head would explode from the sheer delight. The man clearly did not like her. Of course, all that had changed when he saw Devon, still bleeding from the cut on his face, slide out of the driver's seat.

"What in the world is going on here?" he demanded, grabbing his son roughly by the arm and pulling him away from the car.

Devon tried and failed to stifle a pained gasp as his newly cracked ribs rejected the notion of forced movement.

Unfortunately, instead of feeling the automatic paternal concern that he probably should have, this just set the Dean off even more. "What happened to you?" His eyes fixed on Rae, standing silently behind. "Did she do this?" When Devon shook his head, his teeth pressed tightly to keep from crying out, the Dean groaned. "What did she get you into now?"

"Dad, stop," Devon muttered, pulling himself gingerly free. "Rae didn't do anything. It wasn't her fault."

The Dean practically bared his teeth as he shot Rae a disgusted look. "It never is, is it?"

"Please," Devon tried to divert him again, "let's not do this right now. Julian needs the infirmary. There's something going on with his visions."

The headmaster's eyes shot to Julian for a split second. "Is that true?"

Julian's eyes were fixed depressingly on the street as he half-slumped against the car. "Yeah, I guess so." His voice was barely audible.

"And what about you?" The Dean clapped his son on the shoulder and noted every detail as Devon pulled back in pain. "What aren't you telling me? What happened to you?"

"Just a few bruised ribs," Devon tried to smile casually, "it's no big deal."

"No big deal?!" his father shouted. "How many times am I going to find you sneaking out with this girl only to come back more broken than when you left? Meanwhile, I see Miss Kerrigan over there doesn't have a scratch—"

A throat cleared sharply and he fell embarrassingly silent as Madame Elpis stepped forward.

"Perhaps, Dean Wardell, you can continue this discussion with your son and his ailing friend in the infirmary. As you well know, any members of Aumbry House are under my jurisdiction."

"Fine." Even the Dean wasn't going to argue with Miss Crow tatù. "Very good Madame Elpis. See that they're suitably punished for this lapse. Both of them," he added hastily, although it was very clear who he meant.

"Detention," Elpis announced briskly. "And a permanent mark on your file. It will be served in the old history building at seven a.m. sharp. Now I suggest you ladies get to bed. If you're even a second late, you'll have to serve it twice. And I'm calling your parents. Or uncle. Or whoever I'm supposed to contact."

"Yes ma'am," Molly and Rae muttered in unison as they followed their house leader back across the lawns. Rae chanced a look at Devon as they swept past, but he kept his eyes fixed on the ground, bracing himself for whatever 'discussion' his father had in mind.

And now here they were. Sitting in a classroom. Punished for their act of selfless bravery in the most elementary way possible.

Julian and Devon were sitting with them as well, just to pass the time. Of course, as they were no longer students they couldn't be subjected to student rules, but they chose to be supportive in their own discreet way. Much to the approval of Madame Elpis, who probably saw it as a latent act of contrition.

Rae rolled her eyes as Elpis, sitting at the front desk, looked meaningfully at the clock and smirked at their confinement. Walking over here this morning with Molly, Rae had the sudden thought that spending an hour or two locked up in a quiet room with her friends wouldn't be so bad. They had a lot to discuss and none of it could be done in a public venue. Then Elpis showed up to 'supervise' and it was clear that they were to sit in silence.

So they did. Each staring off in a different direction. All wasting valuable time.

The door opened suddenly and Rae was pulled from her mind-numbing trance as Carter swept into the room. He took one look at the four spiritless teenagers and threw up his hands in exasperation. "Would someone like to tell me what the hell is going on here?!"

Madame Elpis started to speak but he cut her off.

"First, I hear that there's been some sort of Shawshank break out! Kids throwing themselves out of top-story windows. Then I hear that Julian's in the hospital and that—" He stopped and glowered at each one of the kids in turn. "Would someone like to cue me in?"

"Don't worry, sir, it's all been sorted." The corners of Devon's lips turned up in a hard, disbelieving smile. "We're in *detention*."

Hearing the Privy Council's golden boy cop to such a petty, childish crime just made the situation seem all the more absurd. A vein started throbbing in Carter's neck and Rae wondered if he was having a mild stroke.

"I can see that, Mr. Wardell," Carter growled, "although in the case of yourself and futuristic-boy, I hardly see how that's possible."

"They volunteered to do penance for their misdeeds." Madame Elpis sounded almost proud.

Carter struggled to rein it in. "And what exactly would those misdeeds be?"

"Oh, you know..." In a far cry from his usual respectful manner, Julian kept his gaze fixed blankly on the wall. "Sneaking out, going to movies, messing around." His eyes flashed up to Carter's. "Kid stuff."

More than anything, it was Julian's odd behavior that seemed to push Carter over the edge. He rubbed his forehead, as if battling an oncoming headache, and gestured to Madame Elpis. "Alda, let them go."

She looked scandalized. "But sir! They've only served half their time—"

"And I'm saying to let them go," he cut her off authoritatively. "Miss Skye and Miss Kerrigan have finals to study for, and I'm sure Devon and Julian have better things to do than sit here in this abandoned classroom staring at the cracks in the wall."

Julian shrugged casually. "Not really..." Devon kicked him under the desk.

Carter studied them all for a second, before pointing impatiently to the door. "That's it, get out of here—go! Study, train, do whatever it is you're doing to fill your time. And don't waste mine!"

Rae didn't wait for him to change his mind. She got up and Molly followed her with the boys trailing after. Rae hurried out the door without a second glance at either Carter of Elpis. She couldn't tell exactly why she was annoyed with Carter in particular, but it seemed there was some sort of cosmic injustice in the double-standard they'd been forced into with the stupid detention and being sent back to Guilder for exams. She'd been out in the field, she had experience bigger than what she could learn in some books. Right?

Risk your lives. Fight to the death. Track down serial killers.

Except...

Now there were finals, curfews, and detentions. Infantile punishments for serious acts.

Carter and the PC, as well as their parents and school, couldn't have it both ways. Either they were kids, to be treated as such, or they were fully grown with the responsibility and respect that came with that position. Guilder had to choose. They *all* had to choose.

As they filed outside, Carter called as he leaned against the doorframe, "Miss Kerrigan, your mother wanted me to remind you she's hosting another dinner tonight. You're expected to come."

Molly rolled her eyes. "Have fun with that, Rae."

"Actually," Carter gave Molly a piercing stare, "let's call this one family *and* friends, shall we? It seems we all have a lot of catching up to do. See you at seven."

The four of them nodded wordlessly and set out across the lawn. Instead of going back to Rae's dorm to study, they headed straight for the Oratory without even asking each other if they wanted to go.

The Oratory was quiet. Rae shivered as she stepped in. The hallway was cool and she knew the large Oratory training room would be cooler. This was where Lanford spent most of his time, where Kraigan had tried to kill her and nearly succeeded, where she had learned about her tatù. There were good memories but each one seemed to be connected with one that reminded her how much her life had changed. She pushed her shoulders back and straightened. She wouldn't let her thoughts push her down.

"So, what happened to you last night?" Rae asked Julian as she reached for a pointed spear and threw it at a target on the wall. "Did the doctors check you out?"

"I'm fine." He threw his spear a bit harder than necessary and it shattered upon impact. "Oops."

Rae glanced at the shards on the floor before returning her gaze cautiously to her friend. "I have trouble with my tatùs sometimes," she said tentatively. "It gets hard to balance—"

"My problem isn't balance," he said abruptly and drilled another spear at the target. "It's control."

They continued throwing until they ran out of spears and out of reasons to avoid eye contact, so Julian turned to her with a sigh.

"I got caught in a wave. Every miniscule decision all four of you were making," he gestured with his hands, "I was seeing all of them."

Molly picked up the spears that weren't broken and brought them back to Rae and Julian. "At least you were getting the full picture..."

"No, it was much more than that." He shook his head helplessly and rubbed his eyes. "Every time you decided to take a step, Molls. Every time Rae debated when to rush into the fight. Every time Kraigan wondered whether or not he was actually going to pull the trigger. Hundreds of minute decisions happening all at the same time. I couldn't pull out of it. It felt like I was drowning."

Devon set down a pair of throwing knives and then shoved them to the side like he didn't have any interest in using them. "What did the doctor say? I mean, after my dad and I left your room."

There was something about his tone that lent an ominous ring to the simple sounding words and both boys exchanged a swift look.

"He said I was in temporary shock," Julian replied. "Something similar to a neurological overload."

Rae bit her lip. It didn't sound good at all. "Is there anything they can do? Some kind of—"

"Nope," he cut her off with a forced smile. "There's nothing they do. It's just something I have to work out on my own. I'll get there." He sighed. "Just have to figure it out."

Devon clapped him casually on the shoulder. "You will, man."

"Sure," Julian replied easily, but in his eyes there was a flicker of doubt.

The conversation dropped as the four of them split off to their separate corners of the room to work. Molly was blasting smoking holes in a group of mannequins, likely imagining Kraigan with every blast. Julian was setting about picking up the broken pieces of his shattered spears, and Devon started climbing a rope hanging in the far corner. While most people opted to curl their legs around and use their feet for leverage, he was dangling in mid-air, using only his hands.

Switching to Devon's own tatù, Rae quickly scampered up a rope that was beside his. "Hey."

It was hard to get the drop on a guy like Devon, but he was so lost in his thoughts that he hadn't even heard her come up. "Rae!" He almost lost his grip entirely, hanging now by one hand.

"Sorry," she laughed quietly, offering her hand. "I didn't mean to scare you."

"You didn't scare me." He grinned and tightened his grip. "I was just...thinking."

Rae steeled herself. "About your dad?"

Devon's eyes flickered to hers before he deflected. "About Julian."

Rae spotted the lie, but let it pass. "I'm sorry if I got you in trouble last night. It looked like he was coming down pretty hard on you."

"*You* didn't get me in trouble," he said quickly. "I can make my own choices."

"I know that." She swung up her legs so she was sitting on top of the bar that ran across the length of the high ceiling, dangling her legs fifty feet above Julian and Molly's heads. "I just know your dad doesn't like me very much, so I—"

"Hey!" He jumped up next to her and put his hand over hers. "He has nothing to do with us. Okay? It's just you and me. We are the only two people in this relationship."

Rae smiled in spite of herself. "It's still so strange to hear you call us a relationship."

He chuckled. "Well, I certainly hope it's a relationship. Otherwise, I'd feel pretty mixed up about what we've been doing these last couple of nights."

"What?" Rae teased him. "You don't go hunting down psychopaths for girls you aren't dating?"

He pressed his forehead against hers and grinned. "I don't make it a custom to have sex with girls I'm not dating."

She blushed and glanced automatically around. "Okay, since for the time being we're living at a school full of people with superhuman abilities, how about you at least lower your voice?!"

He laughed again. "Oh, come on. Who's going to hear?"

At that moment, the door banged open and a class of first year students poured inside. They spotted Devon and Rae immediately on the ceiling bar and many of them pointed in astonishment.

"Do you see them?!"

"How cool is that!"

"How on earth are they going to get down?"

Rae glanced back at Devon and rolled her eyes. "Oh, I don't know. *Them*?"

Devon winked at her. "See ya at the bottom." He slipped off the bar and let his body fall. Rae immediately followed, tightening her body so she could beat him to the ground. They landed on their feet on the floor and both of them rolled in a somersault to absorb the impact. It was as if they had planned it perfectly.

The first years erupted into hand claps and cat calls. Rae curtsied and Devon bowed before they headed to the hall where Molly and Julian were waiting. On the way out, Ellie, the young girl from the library, caught Rae's attention once more.

"Hey! Are we still on for our group mentoring Tuesday?"

"Uh, yeah." With the whole Kraigan fiasco, Rae had almost completely forgotten. "Every Tuesday, that's what we said, right?" She winked. "I'll see you then."

Leaving the over-excited class behind, Rae and Molly split off from the boys and headed back across the lawns to Aumbry House. They still had an afternoon of studying to look forward to before what promised to be another eventful family dinner.

"I just don't understand why you got detention," Beth said for the third time as she passed around a plate of mashed potatoes. Their plates were already heaped full, but ever the mother, Beth kept on adding. "James?" She turned to him, expecting some sort of response.

Rae mimicked the gesture, taking no small amount of pleasure in watching Carter squirm.

"Technically speaking, Molly and Rae are still students here at Guilder." He sounded apologetic. "We need to follow the school rules accordingly, all students have to graduate. Rae understands that...don't you, Rae?"

Rae held his gaze for a moment before shrugging a shoulder. "Sure. How come we can't just test out? I thought that's what you said when I signed the contract and found out you were the pre—" She stopped short when Carter sent her a look of warning. Not everyone knew he was the president of the PC council. Molly probably didn't know. Only a few did. There was danger in numbers.

"While we're on the subject," Beth turned to her shrewdly, oblivious of the exchange between Rae and Carter, "what *were* you doing? And don't tell me you went all the way out to London to go on some sort of midnight double date, because we flat out won't believe you."

Molly and Julian flashed each other an appraising look, then shrugged in concordance.

"We were..." Rae trailed off nervously. With her Uncle Argyle living half a world away, she wasn't used to seeking parental permission before she went off and risked her neck. "We kind of...met up with..." She glanced around, hoping to get some support from her friends. Seeing that wasn't going to happen, she met her mother's tough stare. "I went to see my half-brother, Kraigan."

Carter slammed his fist down on the table. "Are you out of your mind?!"

Beth's face grew pale. "Didn't you say he was the one who tried to *kill* you? Wasn't it his mother in the fire?"

"He's a lunatic!" Carter roared, clearly ticked off. "Dangerous and psychotic! What in the world possessed you to think seeking him out was a smart idea?" he growled. "And you wonder why we treat you like children!"

"We sought him out for precisely those reasons you both just said," Rae answered calmly, keeping her eyes on her mother's face. "He's a dangerous psychopath whose mother died in the fire." She pointedly moved her gaze over to Carter. "The fire that *Jennifer* caused. The rogue, undercover black op agent of the PC's."

There was a moment of silence as the adults absorbed this, then Carter shook his head emphatically. "Oh Rae, you can't be serious."

"Think about it," Devon came to her defense, "who better to catch a killer, than a killer?"

"Kraigan can't be controlled," Carter insisted. "He's a loose cannon. There's no telling who he might turn on."

"Ironically, it was you who let him out of prison." Rae stood her ground, refusing to believe her decision had been a bad one. "I'm not trying to control him. I simply pointed him in the right direction. No one has a greater reason to want Jennifer brought to justice than him. Isn't that what we all want," she glanced around the table, "to take Jennifer down?"

Beth, at least, seemed to accept her daughter's reasoning, but she was still concerned with the belated risk. "He could have killed you," she muttered reproachfully. "He could've seriously hurt any one of you. Or all of you. You need to think about these things before you go gallivanting off without—"

"Without what?" Rae interrupted, a bit more sharply than she'd been intending. She threw her napkin on the table. "Without asking permission?" Her eyes flickered to Carter. "Going after Kraigan is nothing the PC themselves haven't asked me to do before."

Carter opened his mouth to reply, but fell short, reaching for his wine glass instead.

Beth, however, was hardly satisfied. "I know how the PC works. I was one of them. The point is, you could've gotten hurt. How am I supposed to be okay with that?" Her eyes flew accusingly around the table.

"Mom, we're all fine. I told you, it's no big—"

"No big deal?" Beth demanded, mimicking her daughter with the napkin toss. "Don't think I don't see Devon eating with his left hand, when I know he favors his right. Cracked ribs, right?"

He met her gaze guiltily and she nodded. "I've certainly had those before. And what's this I hear about Julian going to the hospital?"

Molly jumped in helpfully. "That was unrelated."

"Julian?" Beth asked sharply. Rae and her friends had quickly found that Beth's maternal instincts were not just limited to her own child.

Julian's dark eyes flashed up to hers, but he merely shrugged. "It was unrelated."

Beth leaned back, but this time, it was Carter who couldn't let it go. "That's not what Dr. Leventhal told me. He said you got lost in some kind of trance."

"It wasn't a trance." Julian's face paled and he stared down at his plate. "I don't want to talk about it," he said softly.

Carter proceeded carefully. "You should know, there have been other cases of—"

"I don't want to talk about it!"

Rae was stunned. Julian could always, *always* be counted on to be the most level-headed member of their group. He was the one she went to for advice, and she had seen the 'adults' in a situation turn to him for assurance or council many times. His words were careful and absolute. To hear him mouth off like this to Carter, she didn't know what to make of it.

Rather than get angry, Carter's face softened as he regarded the young man across the table from him. "Julian, that's a hell of a gift you were given. One of the strongest of them all. No one expects you to handle it alone."

"But I am," Julian's eyes flashed though his voice remained soft, "...handling it. Can we just let it go? Please?"

Devon cleared his throat and picked up his fork. "How about we eat some of this dinner that Beth made before it gets cold?"

The rest of dinner carried on in relative silence. Hardly more than a 'please, pass the salt'. As they cleared the plates, the boys started putting their shoes on.

"I can do the dishes, girls," Beth said quietly.

Neither Rae nor Molly argued with her. Rae had spent most of dinner wondering how everything had gotten out of control. How these grownups could act like they knew everything when they didn't understand it at all. Her mom hadn't been with tatùs for over ten years. She couldn't just jump back in like she was ready to fight and be the super hero-agent she had been. Rae knew her mom wasn't trying to. She just needed someone to direct her anger at.

Beth walked with them outside while Carter remained in the cottage. "Rae. Devon. Julian. Molly." She said each name as if each of them were her child.

They all paused and turned around to look at her.

She smiled slightly, lines on her forehead showed the worry she was trying to hide. "Whether you realize it or not, the four of you have come to a crossroad. It's familiar to me, but you have yet to cross it."

"What do you mean?" Julian asked politely as he clearly didn't understand like the rest of them.

"You've come to a point at which your own power and independence has grown too great to ignore. A point at which you will either have to sink or swim." Beth wrapped her shawl around her shoulders. "But either way, it's a decision you will have to make alone." She smiled tenderly at each of them before turning to go inside.

"What does she mean?" Molly asked. "I don't swim, I'm electrical. I could kill everyone in the pool, or all the fish in a lake. It's too dangerous. For everyone."

"Crap!" Rae slapped her forehead.

"What?" Devon moved instantly beside her. "What's wrong?"

"She's like my Uncle Argyle," she replied.

"What do you mean?"

Rae rolled her eyes. "She speaks in proverbs of truths too."

Chapter 9

Days stretched into weeks stretched into months with the same routine. Finals were looming closer than ever, and most days, Rae locked herself away in the library with the rest of her class to study. In the rare moments she wasn't there, she went to the Oratory, training and sparring with anyone who was available. She felt a deep sympathy for Julian's ongoing struggle to get a handle on his powers, but she was also intensely jealous he'd been able to progress his gift as far as he had. Although her time was limited and her nerves were already stretched to the brink, she forced herself to do the same—pushing against every boundary she could.

Fridays became family dinner night, evenings devoted to poring endlessly through her mother's files, and every Tuesday, she and her friends headed to the library to mentor the first years.

In the beginning, Rae worried about the mentorship. Helping the kids get a handle on their tatùs was one thing, but how on earth was Cromfield supposed to fit in? As it turned out, it was Carter who solved the problem. During their second week in, he showed up at the library to see how things were progressing, and casually suggested that as part of the children's mandatory historical research papers (something Rae was sure he'd made mandatory just for the occasion), they focus on the origins of Guilder and its founders—specifically, Jonathon Cromfield. The kids were eager to impress, and every moment they weren't paired off working with one of their four mentors, they dedicated themselves to cataloguing Cromfield's every move; tracking down places he went, things he did, countries he visited—anything that could help the gang narrow down the search. Not that they knew there was a search, of course. While Rae and her friends were working tirelessly to find the monster, the kids were simply hoping for a passing grade.

"Hey, it could be worse," Molly whispered to an increasingly discouraged Rae. They had just come in to start the weekly session after yet another fruitless day working with Beth's files. Taking a moment to collect themselves, they paused inside the door and watched the children hunched over books in the library. "We could be on research duty."

"You know what?" Rae rubbed her eyes tiredly. "I'd almost prefer it."

As eager as she'd been to first recover her mother's files from Jennifer's flat, it only took a few times reading through them to discover there wasn't much there. They were just your basic Privy Council mission reports. The dates, locations, and agency objectives showed no obvious pattern and absolutely no connection to Cromfield. The only thing that set them apart from the rest of the PC's database were a series of strange, coded notes written on the side. At first, Rae had thought they were just scribbles, something written in a blurred shorthand by whoever was logging the files into the main database. However, she soon realized there was more to them than met the eye. She and Molly had taken them to Beth, working to decode whatever information they were meant to protect, but they'd made very little progress.

Although the code was something Beth and Jennifer had created together at the height of their PC super-agent hay-day, Jennifer had modified it while Beth was in France. Now, while Beth could understand the basic essence of a phrase, all the details eluded her. She tried her best to help the girls, but so far, all they'd been able to glean from the documents was that no matter where Beth was sent, she kept running into Simon. It was like someone was maneuvering them together, continually positioning them in the same place, at the same time.

Why? Rae had no idea.

"Don't say that," Molly chided gently. "Come on, you're being too hard on yourself. You've been working your butt off, Rae. We all have. If there's something to find, we *will* find it... eventually."

"I know." Rae sighed. "I appreciate everything you, and the guys, are doing to help me track him down, I really do. It's just..." Her eyes flickered out the window, sweeping over the darkened lawns and peacefully shadowed trees.

Molly flashed her a knowing smile. "You wish you were out there hunting with Kraigan."

Rae couldn't help but chuckle. Her friend knew her too well. "Is that weird? I mean, I don't want to be out there with *Kraigan* specifically, but at least he's actively doing something. In the meantime, we're stuck inside, forced to play like we're just ordinary school girls, masking this mission. One that should be top PC priority. Instead we're acting like we're doing a history project for a bunch of little kids. It's driving me crazy!"

Molly nodded sympathetically, gazing out over the first years and studying them with a critical eye. "Think of it this way, school's almost over. Finals are in just a few weeks, then comes graduation." She poked Rae in the ribs excitedly. "And *then*, you and I can finally ditch this school altogether and move into our apartment."

Frustrations aside, Rae couldn't help but thrill at the idea. It hadn't been that long ago that she was sitting exactly where these kids were sitting themselves. Fresh to Guilder, new to the world of tatùs, completely unaware of the path that lay before her. Not to mention the fact that she would soon fall head over heels in love with the boy assigned to be *her* mentor.

But so many things had happened since those first days. First, there'd been Lanford, his stinging betrayal as she lay chained in a stone dungeon, listening to the psychotic ramblings of her father. Then there'd been Kraigan—Devon's brutal kidnapping, their fight to the death in a burning factory. The more time went by, the more things kept piling up. Jennifer's hidden agenda, Luke's coma, and Rae's constant uphill battle against being labeled a hybrid pariah.

Yes, it hadn't been that long since she'd been sitting in those seats herself. Yet she was a whole different person from when she'd started at Guilder. When she looked in the mirror now, there was hardly a trace of the innocent, trusting girl who'd first walked through these halls.

She'd adapted. She had to if she wanted to stay alive. These days, she was quicker to action, slower to trust. And while she may have picked up Charles' ability to perpetually heal, she carried around the scars from every fight, every betrayal, every time she'd been let down by those people who were meant to protect her.

"I'm thinking of doing the walls in a light powder blue," Molly was thinking aloud, oblivious to her friend's dark reverie. "Nothing gaudy, of course, just a touch of color to make the space seem bigger than it is and liven it up a little. I actually already ordered the curtains to match. Of course, the accent walls will be a different story altogether..."

Rae looked up in surprise and smiled fondly at her best friend. Of course, not everything that happened since she came to Guilder was bad. In fact, despite the annual catastrophes that seemed to shake her to the core, she'd made some of the happiest memories of her life on this campus. Come into herself as a person, reconnected with her long-lost mother. Been introduced to a group of people that would serve to be life-long friends.

"...and I don't want you to freak out, but I'm thinking the first thing we're going to have to do is re-tile. I know it sounds like a lot of work, but I don't want to look back in five months and think: if we just hadn't cut corners..."

Rae chuckled to herself and led a continuously-babbling Molly into the library.

Yep—Guilder had a way of balancing the good with the bad.

"Rae, hi!" Cassidy, the girl with the unique ability to make herself invisible, came bounding across the library, her presence revealed only by the pile of books she accidently knocked off the table. "Are we going to get a chance to work one-on-one again today? I've been practicing!"

Rae laughed. "I can see that!"

Molly shook her head sarcastically. "I can't..." Cassidy flashed back into sight and laughed as Molly jumped away in surprise. "I'll leave you freaks to it," she teased, recovering herself. "I have a protégé to groom."

With that, she flounced off across the room to meet with Noah, the boy who shared her power of electricity. He greeted her with an over-excited wave, grimacing apologetically when the accompanying shower of sparks set a row of books on fire.

"Caleb, put that out please." Devon walked calmly into the library, directing a boy with water abilities towards the source of the flame. "Hey babe—Rae. Hey Rae," he corrected himself as he joined Rae by a worktable.

"No Julian today?" Rae glanced at the door and listened for Julian in the hall.

There was a hitch in Devon's breathing before he shook his head casually. "Nope. He decided to stay in tonight. Had some stuff he wanted to work on."

He exchanged a quick look with Rae. These days, Julian seemed to be spending more and more time inside, locked away in his room as he battled for control of his visions. Rae had been worried he was hiding more drawings of her but he vehemently denied it. Devon, Rae and Molly tried to help, showing up with food and volunteering to sit as test dummies as he experimented different ways to keep himself in the present. After a few weeks of persistent disappointment, he'd started avoiding them altogether. At this point, Rae and Devon had actually gone to Carter for council, but all Carter would say was that Julian had been given an incredibly powerful gift, and it was up to him to master it on his own. The rest of them had to be patient and supportive.

Rae had found Carter's advice to be a completely unacceptable solution, but before she could once again voice her concerns to Devon, they were startled by a small shriek coming from behind a stack of books. They raced over in alarm, only to see Ellie crouched over a dusty volume that looked like it weighed as much as she did, raising her hands in victory.

"I knew it!" she exclaimed, shoving the book towards a sullen-looking Ethan. "Cromfield was back in London in 1535. He was seen leaving St. Stephen's Church after a midnight mass. I freaking told you so!"

Rae stared at her. Ellie found a mention of Cromfield. It wasn't much, but it was a start. Better than nothing.

"How on earth did you remember that?" Ethan complained. "Chapter, page, and line number—verbatim? It's impossible!"

Ellie's face tensed for a fraction of a second, before she held out her hand. "Maybe I'm just smarter than you. Either way, you owe me five pounds."

He rolled his eyes, then smirked as he held an open palm up in the air. A moment later, a crisp five-pound note shimmered into view. He slapped it into Ellie's hand, who pocketed it with a smug, "Thank *you*!"

"Hey!" Devon chided Ethan. "You know what I said about creating money. Super powers or not, you're still a tax-paying citizen of this country, and I don't want to get a phone call from the Secretary of the Treasury one day about a slew of unmarked bills. Tone it down!"

"Dude," Ethan said dismissively, "I'm fourteen. I don't pay taxes."

Devon didn't blink. "Rae, do you still have Prince Philip's private cell number? I have a future felon I'd like to report."

Rae grinned as Ethan held up his hands and sprang away from the table. "Okay, okay! I won't make any more money." He paused suddenly and bit his lip. "What about...pizza?"

"Oh, bring on the pizza," Devon encouraged, clearing a space in the center of the table.

There was a group cheer around the library as the heavy smell of pepperoni and cheese wafted through the air. A second later, everyone was gathered around the table—loading slices onto plates.

Rae watched them with a faint grin, but stayed fixed in place, fingers still touching the page Ellie had just found. She wished there was more information here but it was just a sighting. That was it. She smiled, appreciating Devon's form of distraction with the rest of the class so she could focus on what Ellie had found. No one knew how key this information could be. Rae wasn't sure either. It wasn't much. At all.

St. Stephen's Church?...Where had she heard that name before?

"Kerrigan," Ethan called, holding out a plate. "You want one too?"

Devon shrugged at her helplessly, unable to come up with something to cover her. Rae glanced down at the book again with a slight frown before getting up and joining the rest of her friends.

"Yeah...I'm coming."

Chapter 10

"Molly, this is so far out of our price range, it's ridiculous!"

Molly and Rae stood on the sidewalk on a wintery London morning, looking up at the gleaming balcony of a penthouse apartment five stories above. While Rae had compiled a list of more modest options for their search, Molly had driven them straight here, double parking and gazing up at the luxury suite with open arms.

"We have no price range," she insisted. "We're freaking secret agents, Rae! Live a little!"

"I plan to live a little," Rae countered, tugging her friend back towards the car, "I just don't plan to live *there*."

"Oh come on," Molly begged, planting her feet on the ground. "At least come up and look at it! I already reserved this time with the property manager for our viewing."

"You did?" Rae asked with a frown. Molly flushed like she'd given something away, and something suddenly clicked. "Molly! You already put down the security deposit, didn't you?"

Molly bit her lip and smiled nervously. "...Maybe?"

"*Molly Elizabeth Skye!*"

"What was I supposed to do?!" she defended herself anxiously. "The realtor said it was only going to be on the market for a couple of days! We had to pounce!"

Rae looked up again at the balcony. "We had to pounce on one of the priciest flats in all of London?!"

"I heard Devon and Julian are thinking of moving in down the street."

There was a pause.

"Let's go up and take a look."

The apartment was everything Rae could have ever imagined and more. It reminded her of Heath Hall, where she had stayed with Devon in order to protect the future Queen. This place though, was so much more. After one look, she instantly decided 'the apartment' was too lackluster a name. The *penthouse* was a top story suite that connected two separate bedrooms, each with their own bathroom, with a wide kitchen and living space that lay in the center. The front door opened up to a common area, but it was unlike any living room Rae had ever seen. Dark hardwood floors stretched from the luxurious sitting area all the way to the far wall, which wasn't a wall at all, but a massive sheet of spotless glass that opened up onto an outdoor patio with a view overlooking the city. The kitchen was already decked with every appliance known to man, a bit superfluous as neither Rae nor Molly knew how to cook, and a tall closet lay just past the front door, complete with its own coat rack.

"Okay..." Rae took a tentative step inside, "this is..."

Molly shadowed her every movement, hanging on every word as she tried to gauge her friend's reaction.

"I mean..." Rae sank down onto one of the leather couches and flipped her dark hair over the side, peering up at the antique chandelier that hung from the ceiling. "Molly, you know how sometimes you get into those moods where you order some insanely expensive clothes, and the next day I guilt you about cost and impulsivity?"

Molly's face fell as her eyes welled with emotion. "...Yeah?"

"This is *not* one of those times."

The flaming redhead did a double take. "Wait—what?"

Rae grinned. "I love it."

"*You do?!*"

Molly streaked across the room in a whirl of crimson and Burberry. "Thank bloody goodness! I've been so excited to show you, but I wasn't sure if you'd approve because of the price!"

"Speaking of, that would be...?"

"It doesn't matter," Molly said in a casual dismissal. "You know, you still get paid even when you're on probation from the PC, and needless to say, just one of our first paychecks was more than enough to cover first and last month's rent."

Rae looked around the room in awe. "I just can't believe this. I can't believe that we can actually live in a place like this. It doesn't seem possible."

She had grown up in relative privilege living with her Uncle Argyle. Back when Beth was presumed dead, she had left Rae a sizable inheritance. But it was not to be touched until she turned twenty-five, so Rae had always assumed that until that time, she would have to make ends meet on her own. Except now, her mother was alive and that money belonged to her. Rae didn't need it. Her job would cover whatever expenses she had. Realistically she could ask any amount she wanted; the PC would be idiots to say no. She was one of their most valuable assets. She smiled at the thought. She wouldn't be greedy, but she would be fair.

She stroked the soft cashmere draping the sofa. She must have walked past this block in London many times, but she never for one second imagined that she might actually end up here. And the fact that Devon might be moving in just down the street...?

"Well, you'd better believe it, sister!" Molly squealed, grabbing her hand and pulling her up for the full tour. "Because I've already signed the paperwork!"

While Molly had opted for the room with a full city view and the bigger walk-in closet, Rae was actually quite pleased with her private balcony's view of the quiet city park that lay just across the street. They were about as centralized in the city as they could be, but because of the exclusive residential boundaries, the streets were picturesque and serene. Between that and the gigantic bathtub that could realistically fit about five people, Rae had found a home.

"Okay first obstacle," she said when she eventually peeled herself away from the walk-in shower, "we need to graduate, like, *now*."

Molly nodded fervently, holding up color swatches against the wall. "I hear you. I wish there was some way we could opt to finish the year off-campus and just move now."

Rae sighed but shook her head. "As fantastic as that sounds, I think we're both where we need to be right now at Guilder. There's so much going on, and what with the mentoring and my mom—"

"Say no more." Molly held up her hand. "It's going to take me at least a month to figure out my decorating scheme anyway."

Rae chuckled. "Do I have any say in that part or—" Molly flashed her a caustic look and she fell silent. "Yeah, that's what I figured."

"Come on," Molly grinned, "let's sign your paperwork and get some celebratory lunch. I'm thinking...sushi."

When they rode the elevator back downstairs, they were greeted profusely by a lobby attendant named Raphael. It seemed that as excited as Rae and Molly were about the apartment complex, the complex was just as excited to be adding them. It wasn't very often that two, young, attractive girls could afford a place in this neighborhood on their own, and news had travelled fast.

"Miss Skye!" Raphael greeted her like an old friend. "It's so good to see you again!" They kissed on both cheeks before he turned his beaming gaze to Rae. "And this must be the lovely Miss Kerrigan we've been hearing so much about."

"The one and only," Rae said a little awkwardly, flashing Molly a look as he pulled her in for the double-cheek kisses as well. Over-enthusiastic as he might be, she had to admit, it was nice to be somewhere where her last name didn't strike fear into the heart of the community. Maybe this move was going to be even better-timed than she'd thought.

"I've already pulled up the rental agreement, and thanks to Miss Skye's deposit and credit history, that's really the only information we need. That and your ID."

"Sure," Rae said, pulling out her driver's license and signing below Molly's name on the dotted line.

Only a few seconds later, the entire transaction was complete. She and Molly skipped out the door arm in arm, brand new residents of a posh London penthouse.

"To our soon-to-be home!" Molly raised her mini-espresso in cheers and they clinked over a plate of sashimi and rolls. "May it prove less hazardous than our last home, but just as fun!"

"I'll drink to that!"

They downed their coffees in one shot, and Rae was quick to order two more.

"And speaking of fun..." Molly looked at her with a sly twinkle, battling a piece of salmon with her chopstick. "You never did say what you thought about Devon moving in basically next door."

Rae flushed and dropped her eyes to the table, letting her dark curls spill between them like a shield. "Well, I actually...um, I think it will, um..." She smothered a grin. "Yeah, that'll rock—I mean that'll work."

Both girls burst out giggling as their new drinks arrived. The steam didn't do anything to help cool Rae's cheeks as she took another scalding gulp.

"Not that it matters much anyway," Molly said in the same mischievous tone, "you and Devon are practically living together as it is."

"What?" Rae tossed a napkin at her. "That's so not true!"

"Oh come on!" Molly giggled. "You don't think I've noticed how your guys' late night work sessions, turn into...all night sessions? You just better be careful that Madame Elpis doesn't see him sneaking out every morning. I think she'd have a stroke."

Rae chuckled a little nervously and poked at her food. Were they being that obvious? Carter and their closest friends might know about their relationship, but that *did not* mean that it was in any way sanctioned by either the school, the PC, or even the tatù community at large. There were centuries' worth of traditional and precedent they were flouting, and who knew how serious the consequences might prove if they were caught? If Devon's own father's reaction was any indicator, they would be dire indeed...

"You're right," Rae murmured, "we should be more careful."

Molly's eyes softened sympathetically. "Only for a little while. And then," she said as she tossed her hair back casually, "you know, we're moving into this amazing penthouse."

Both girls kept up the cool façade for only a moment before they erupted once more in little shrieks of joy. The waiter placed their check on the table with a judgmental eye roll, and they stifled their giggles behind their hands as Rae set down some cash.

"So, how about it Molls?" she asked as they walked back to the car. "Time to get back to the grindstone?"

There was a pause in Molly's step and she faltered. "Um, actually...I kind of..."

Rae stopped walking at once and rubbed her arms to keep warm. "What is it? Why are you being so weird?"

Molly seemed to be having trouble keeping eye contact. "I actually have a date. With Luke."

An ill-timed gust of icy wind swept down between them and Rae took a step back. "Oh!" she said softy, blinking in surprise. "I see."

Molly's pale skin flushed as pink as her scarf. "Are you mad? Rae, please don't be mad. I thought that since you and Devon are such a firmly established couple, and nothing really ever went anywhere with Luke, that it would be okay."

Rae took a deep breath, but her friend cut her off before she could start talking.

"Oh, I knew it! You are mad. That's fine. You have every right to be. I don't even know what I was thinking. I'll just call him right now and cancel. You're my best friend. I don't want anything to come between—"

"Molly!" Rae took her by the shoulders and grinned. "It's all right. I'm cool with it."

Molly stopped mid-sentence, looking like someone had knocked the wind right out of her sails. "You are? I mean, are you *really*? Or is this one of those things where in fifty years you'll kill my dog and be like, 'What did you expect? You dated Luke'."

Rae threw back her head and laughed. She was willing to bet that in fifty years she still wouldn't even be close to understanding how Molly's mind worked. "I'm *seriously* okay with it," she assured her. "Better than okay. Why wouldn't I be? You're my best friend in the whole world, and Luke's one of the best guys I've ever met. You guys would make an awesome pair."

Molly closed her eyes and sank down onto a bench on the sidewalk. "You have no idea how relieved I am to hear you say that." She sighed. "I've been mulling it over for weeks, trying to figure out how to tell you."

"Weeks?!" Rae exclaimed, sitting down beside her. "You kept this from me for weeks?!"

Molly's eyes narrowed accusingly. "Do you really want to play who-kept-their-relationship-a-secret-the-longest?"

"Fair point."

They laughed softly at the irony as Molly pulled out her car keys and began fiddling them between her fingers. "The thing is...I really like him. I mean, *really* like him. I was thinking of asking him to be my date to graduation."

Rae wrapped her arm around Molly's tiny shoulders. "Then I'm *really* happy for you. Who knows? Maybe Luke will switch sides, join up with the PC, and become Julian and Devon's third roommate."

"Ha!" Molly snorted. "Yeah, that wouldn't be awkward at all. Just one big happy family."

Rae grinned and got to her feet. "They'll eventually make a TV show about us. They can call it: 'Three Guys, Two Girls...And a Whole Lot of Baggage'."

Molly rolled her eyes. "Occasionally guest starring the Royal Family." She pulled out her phone to call Luke and handed Rae the car keys. "If you don't mind driving back, I can just have him drop me off."

"Sounds good." Rae tossed her purse inside and was just sliding into the driver's seat when she suddenly paused. "Hey, Molls?"

Molly looked up from her phone. "Yeah?"

"I really am happy for you."

They beamed at each other a moment before Molly said, "I'm happy for us both."

The drive back to Guilder seemed to take no time at all, and Rae was still riding the high of the apartment when she started walking up the deserted stairs of Aumbry. She'd almost made it to the top when the sound of muffled crying made her pause. Silent as a ghost, she flitted back to the front door and traced the noise to a little tuft of hair sticking up from behind one of the sofas in Aumbry House's library.

"Ellie?" she asked incredulously. "Is everything okay?"

The little girl jumped and looked up at Rae with a tear-stained face. At first, she tried to shrug it off, but a gasping sob rocked her tiny body and she shook her head, burying her face in her knees. Rae sank to the ground beside her, stroking back her hair and wondering what on earth could be the matter. Had there been a death in the family? Was it just the stress of school?

"Sweetie," she said after a few moments, "you want to tell me what's going on?"

Ellie pulled in a shaky breath and peered up at her. "I d-do, but I just d-don't know what's going to h-happen. I d-don't want to—" She choked on another wave of tears.

Rae patted her soothingly on the back, the way Devon had comforted her so many, many times before. "I'm not going to repeat anything you tell me unless you want me to," she murmured in a low voice. "I'm your friend here. Not your teacher, not campus police."

Ellie looked up tentatively, but again, her face crumbled and she shook her head.

With the air of someone who had all the time in the world, Rae stretched out her legs on the ground beside her. "That's okay, we can just sit." Ellie nodded a little, and the two of them sat there for almost twenty minutes before Rae tried talking again. "Did you rob a bank?"

Ellie's head shot up with a look of shock. "Wh-what?"

Rae held up her hands. "Hey, no judgment if you did. I've certainly done my share of international larceny, so trust me, I get it."

The young girl just looked on in amazement, but the corners of her lips began to twitch up into a smile.

"Okay, so, no bank robbery." Rae tilted back her head and tried again. "Did you...accidently blow somebody up? Because if you did, I, for one, can testify that Guilder's chemistry lab is woefully outdated—"

"I got my tatù."

All teasing stopped and Rae gazed at her in surprise. It was probably the most emotionally trying ordeal any inked teenager would ever go through. The pressures of which Rae understood intimately. She reached out and squeezed Ellie's hand.

"It...wasn't the one you wanted?"

Ellie sighed shakily and pulled up the back of her shirt.

"That's the problem, it's not just one."

An exquisitely detailed design shone brightly against the girl's pale skin. The detailed image of a smiling girl resting her hand on a book.

Rae leaned forward in amazement. Her fingers itched to reach out and touch Ellie's skin so she could take the ability and find out what it was. Rae hadn't seen one like it before. It was beautiful, unique and slightly larger than other people's tatùs. Kind of like hers. Rae blinked and sat back.

Ellie's voice fell to a whisper, "It's two."

Five minutes later, Ellie was sitting on Rae's bed, holding a cup of steaming hot chocolate to her lips. She'd looked around in wonder at her mentor's messy, top-story room, and was now quietly recovering from her emotional outburst as Rae sat patiently at the desk.

"How long have you known?" she asked quietly. Ellie looked up and she smiled without judgment or blame. "When Ethan asked you how you were able to remember those things in the library...you knew then, didn't you?"

Ellie set the mug down and sighed. "I turned sixteen about two months ago."

Rae's mouth fell open. "*Two months?*"

"I've been hiding it." Ellie stared down at her hands. "I lied on the forms about my birthdate."

Rae's heart swelled protectively as she looked at the young girl. When she'd first started at Guilder, she'd done the exact same thing. Not for *two months*, but still...

"It's why I was so eager to meet you," Ellie continued. "You were the only other person I'd ever met who had two different sets of ink. I thought...I don't know. I thought maybe I could talk to you about it but—"

"But I snapped at you and shut you down," Rae finished.

She remembered quite clearly how little Ellie had come bounding up to her in the library her first day back at school. The girl had been practically begging to get to know her. But that was the same day Rae got her mom back and fought Jennifer. She was in no state to be meeting strangers.

"I'm sorry," she said softly. "I didn't know."

Ellie shrugged dismissively. "Of course not, how could you? Anyway, the longer I kept up the lie, the harder it got to hide it." Her shoulders shook as she sighed again. "All our teachers were always going on about the dangers of mixing powers." Her eyes flickered up to Rae's. "Your name came up a few times. And I don't know, I panicked. I didn't want them to look at me..."

"The way you saw them looking at me."

Ellie nodded and dropped her eyes, afraid she'd offended her.

"It's all right," Rae assured her, flashing her a sad but practical smile. "It is what it is." She decided to turn the conversation on a lighter path. "So, have you figured out what you can do?"

For the first time, Ellie's face lit up with uncontainable excitement. She lifted her shirt again so that Rae could see the ink. It was actually quite beautiful. The girl resting her hand on a book, gazed up, almost as if she was looking at Rae, with a wise smile.

"I think...it lets me understand things," she said slowly. "At first, I thought I was just sharpening up, you know? I mean, I've always been a good student. But the more I learned, the more I realized I was retaining every single thing." She straightened up proudly. "These days, I can read a six hundred-page book start to finish in about five minutes and recite every word."

Rae shook her head slowly. "That's incredible. We have a guy here, Nicholas, we call him MacGyver. He knows how things work, too. But his seems a bit more hands on, technical. Not as book oriented as yours. But who knows? Maybe there's a connection."

"That's not all." Ellie wound her finger up behind her and pointed not at the book, but at the picture of the girl. There was a sparkle in her eyes like she knew more than she was telling. "I know when people are telling the truth."

This time, Rae actually scoffed. "Like a human lie detector?"

Ellie laughed. "I guess so. But it's more like...I know the intention behind things. If I read you a passage from a book, I could tell you what the author was trying to get across, what was going through their head when they wrote it. It applies to people as well, only it's not quite as strong. But I can still pick up on things." She leaned forward conspiratorially. "Like two days ago in class, one of the teachers said that all we'd be doing tomorrow was finishing a movie on the creation of Rome. But she was lying, she's going to make some kind of pop quiz."

Rae leaned back against her chair with a grin. "That's sure handy."

It was like the floodgates had opened. Ellie was over-animated now. Gushing on and on about the different things she was learning how to do. But maybe her gifts were even more useful than she realized. As they were talking, Rae's eyes kept flickering over to the stack of her mother's files, half hidden under a book.

Maybe, just maybe, she should put Ellie's newfound abilities to the test...

Chapter 11

Whoever said, 'with age comes wisdom' had clearly never met Ellie Stratford.

Rae showed Ellie the coded notes scribbled around the edges of the files the next day. She first asked Devon and Beth what they thought. Both were horrified by the idea. Ellie was just a child, after all. No telling what she might do with the information or whom she might tell. But as Rae so patiently reminded them, she herself was just a child when she squared off against Lanford, and through nothing but force of mind remained immune to her father's brainwashing device.

"Don't underestimate a sixteen-year-old girl," she told Devon and her mom repeatedly. "We're stronger than you think."

In the end, they'd come around, but Devon insisted on one thing: all the messages were to be scrambled and out of context. Then Beth insisted that she and Devon would need to be there as well. Rae could just imagine what Ellie would think of the two of them hovering over her head, watching for any sign of trouble she might have.

They needn't have bothered.

As it turned out, despite their extreme diligence, Ellie was more than a match for their cautious ways.

"So, these are the coded messages from the secret mission files your backstabbing partner stole from you?" she asked cheerfully the first time they got together at Beth's cottage.

Beth and Devon both whirled around to glare at Rae, but she just held up her hands with a secret smile. "I didn't tell her. Honest."

"Sorry," Ellie flushed as she ran her hand over the papers. "I just sort of know. They were written with a mean spirit. Like a guilty conscience. By someone who had a lot to hide."

Beth's mouth dropped open, but Devon was quicker to recover himself. "Actually, when Rae told us about your tatù and how the two of you were going to train in secret, we dug through the archives to come up with some old practice material for you. I hope it helps."

"No..." Ellie's childlike giggling shattered his careful calm. "You're hoping that I figure out whatever this code is for so that you and your friends can solve an active case."

Devon stammered half-hearted denials before turning again to Rae for help.

"Don't bother, Dev." Rae chuckled. "I wouldn't try lying to her, she's pretty foolproof. It's a particular set of skills I'm dying to get my hands on." She winked at Ellie. In fact, she hadn't asked Ellie for her skill, nor had the young girl offered. Rae refused to steal this one without permission, even if it meant slowing down the case. This girl would be going through what Rae had at sixteen, she of all people had to respect the ink and wait till it was offered to her. She wasn't her father, or Lanford, or Jennifer. She was Rae. Rae Kerrigan.

"I get where you're coming from, and I understand the importance of this project," Ellie assured him seriously. "I promise, you can count on me to keep quiet." She flashed a wry grin that seemed much too old for such a young face. "After all, Rae's keeping my secret, so, I owe her."

Ellie's 'secret' had proved a source of much contention between her and Rae. After that first day when she'd talked in Rae's room, Rae told Ellie her entire story, trying to impress upon her the fact that the only reason she was able to handle her hybrid status, was by sharing it with the people in her life and letting them support her. While Rae had the Kerrigan name working against her, adding extra fuel to the fire—Ellie had her own troubles. She was born into the tatù community, being fully aware of its existence. She'd grown up with the rules and knew full well what could happen to someone if they didn't fit the norm. Then of course, there was also the obvious family tension. As far as Ellie was aware, only her father was inked. That meant that for her entire life, both parents had been lying to her. It wasn't the sort of thing that inspired honesty in her now.

So, considering honesty and understanding were the two new absolutes by which she was starting to live her inked life, it was surprisingly easy for Ellie to maintain the deception. She simply showed people the tatù on the day she'd said was her birthday, and pretended that—while it was certainly rare—it provided her only one ability. After a brief struggle, she'd decided to go with the 'understanding' part and keep the 'human lie detector' to herself. It's more interesting to know when someone's not telling you the truth, if *they* don't know that *you* know, it gives you a lot more options.

"In that case," Beth patted the girl encouragingly on the back, "let's get started."

Watching Ellie work was like watching a brain trust in action. She flipped through the pages only once, and never touched them again having already memorized every word and its location. After that, she leaned back in her chair and stared out the window while her tatù took effect. Her tiny brow crinkled in concentration as her fingers started drumming rhythmically on the desk.

"It's written in Phoenician..." she murmured appreciatively. "An old sea-faring culture that flourished about twenty-five hundred BC." She glanced up at Beth curiously. "You did this?"

Rae and Devon whirled around, but Beth was blushing furiously at the ground. "Jenn and I stumbled across them in an old book. Figured it was a dead language and it would be safe..."

Ellie nodded as her eyes glazed over once more. "But the other girl twisted it..." All at once, she slammed her hand down on the desk, making the other three jump. "Of course! She's using a running key cipher!"

Her revelation was met with three blank stares and it was her turn to blush.

"Ellie," Rae began gently, "remember what we said about things like dead languages and ancient cryptography *not* being common knowledge...?"

Ellie hung her head. "I know, I know." She popped back up with a grin. "A running key cipher is a simple code based on a book. A phrase from the book helps decode a phrase from the page. It's all right here in her notes. The only problem is, we don't know what book she used."

Rae's heart fell. That was it, wasn't it? Jennifer could have used any book to set the cipher. There was no way of knowing which—

"Slaughterhouse Five. By Kurt Vonnegut."

All heads turned to Beth.

Her mouth had thinned into a hard line, but she twisted it up into a smile. "Simon gave that book to Jennifer for Christmas the year before the fire. She loved it. Never put it down."

Devon leaned over to Rae. "Remind me never to get you books for Christmas. Nothing good can come from them."

Rae poked him in the ribs and turned back to her mom. "Well...that's kind of perfect. There has to be a copy in the library. Devon and I can run over and—"

"Don't worry," Ellie was scribbling on a piece of computer paper, "I already read it."

They watched her work for a moment, hand flying across the page, before she abruptly threw down the pencil. Without even glancing down to see what she'd done, she proudly handed it over.

"There you are!" she declared. "All finished." She hopped up from the desk and skipped across the room to the door. "Now if you don't mind, I have a chemistry test to study for." She reached for the door and quickly spun around. "Wait!" She bounded back to the table and grabbed Rae's hand. "Why don't you try and see if you can figure it out?" She let out a silly laugh and jogged back to the half-open door and left.

Beth, Rae, and Devon watched her little ponytail bouncing away until it disappeared down over the path hill. When it had, Beth turned back to them with a slow smile.

"You guys are going to have your hands full with that one! I don't think she has any idea yet of what she's capable of."

Rae stared at her hand and wiggled her fingers as the new tatù flowed through her body. "It's tingling," she mumbled. "I've had Kraigan's ability. It was a cross tatù, like mine, but this... this is different."

"Good or bad?" Devon asked, the concern on his face clearly apparent.

"Not sure yet." Rae took the page and scanned on through. "Okay, it's not helping me here. There's just a lot of...um, gibberish?"

"You're okay? Not mangled from tatù overload?"

She shook her head and laughed. "It doesn't work like that."

"Really? 'Cause I have no idea."

"I'm fine. It's just unique. Apparently, I need some time to try and figure it out. It's a lot more complex than most tatùs."

"Gotchya." Devon grabbed the written book and took over. "It's not gibberish, just...pretty generic stuff. Genealogies of people in the area where Beth's missions took place. Family trees and blood lines. Why would Jennifer need this stuff?"

"Not Jennifer—*Cromfield*," Beth corrected, taking the page. "There's also what looks like a list of ingredients." She scanned down the paper. "Ethanol, midazolam, sodium pentothal...all to be mixed with a compound X. What the hell is this stuff? It looks like some sort of serum?"

"There's something else here, look." Rae pointed down at the page. "Meet SSC." She looked up at the other two. "Who is SSC?"

Devon shook his head blankly while Beth frowned at the page. "I have no idea..."

"Rae!" A sudden voice in her head made her jump. The other two stared at her in surprise.

"Everything okay?" Devon asked, a single eyebrow raised.

Rae slapped her forehead in frustration. *Coming Maria!* "I totally forgot," she hissed. "Study group."

Beth looked at her like she was crazy. Devon scratched at the scruff growing along his jawline. "Maria?"

She nodded.

"Is she here?" Beth stuffed the page quickly into her jacket. "Don't worry about this right now, honey. Focus on your finals—we need you to graduate. Devon and I can handle this."

Rae chuckled. "Maria's in my head. She can talk by brain messaging basically."

"Oh!" her mom replied.

Devon offered Beth his arm. "How about we let Rae go and study, then you and I can hit the library?" He winked at Rae and pretended to blow kisses her way.

Beth accepted Devon's arm with a smile. "Lead the way."

Rae opened her mouth to protest, but knew she couldn't. She switched to Devon's tatù and raced out the door, past them, to her room in Aumbry. She ran past a group of students heading in the same direction and then caught up with Maria just as she was about to knock on Rae's door.

Rae quickly unlocked the door and just as she went to close it behind Maria, seven teenagers burst into her room and instantly made themselves at home, spreading out a small sea of study notes and books.

Great, she thought as she settled down beside them. *Just great.*

What had been weeks before finals turned into mere days, and the study sessions grew more frequent and longer. Even with MacGyver's notes on the previous tests, there was still an incomprehensible amount of work to do, and the study group soon moved to the library so they could spread out.

Rae desperately wished she could figure out Ellie's tatù and save herself all the trouble, but as it turned out, the hybrid ink was much more convoluted and complex than a single ability. Ellie had a month's head-start practice, but Rae figured she needed some time if she wanted to figure it out. So, in the meanwhile, she studied. And studied and studied. During the increasingly sparse breaks she allowed herself to take, she would have training sessions with Ellie (where she consistently coaxed her to tell her parents) or help her mom and Devon try to track down SSC. But for the most part, she lived chained to the library.

It was almost midnight and she was coming back from one of these study sessions, when she heard the muffled shouts of angry voices followed by the hard slamming of a door. She didn't have time to switch tatùs to try and listen. A chill ran up her spine and she froze in place, hovering tentatively in the shadows. Since she'd been at Guilder she knew better than to ignore these kinds of things.

Don't worry Rae, she told herself. *Whatever it is—you'll handle it.*

A pair of footsteps thundered towards her and she raised her hands, bracing herself for whatever new trouble was brewing. She managed to suck in her breath and stay silent when Devon stormed past her in a rage, heading out to the parking lot to his car.

"Devon?" She stepped out of the shadows, surprised that he hadn't noticed her hiding. He wasn't the kind of agent that missed things like that. Unless he was too angry to focus around him.

He whirled around. "What?!"

"What on earth are you..." Her voice trailed off as she saw the look on his face. Over the past years she'd seen Devon tortured, beaten, betrayed, exsanguinated... You name it—she'd seen it. But this...this was unlike anything before.

He looked completely gutted, staring at her with lost, haunted eyes.

Her face paled and she raced to him. "What the hell happened?!"

He visibly fought to contain himself, and tried to play it off with a casual shrug. "Oh, you know... Just having a little talk with my dad." His face hardened and became unreadable.

Rae glared in the direction of the headmaster's office. Of course! She should have known better. "Come on," she wound a protective hand through his and pulled him behind her, "let's get you inside."

Ten minutes later, Devon had yet to crack. Rae had tried every way she knew how to get him to tell her what had happened, but in addition to being a highly trained operative, he was also one of the most stubborn people she'd ever met. Fortunately for her, he was dating the only person more tenacious than himself. "If you don't tell me what's going on," she said as she huffed in exasperation, "I'll use Carter's power on you. And then we'll have this big fight about boundary issues, and even though I was technically in the wrong, *I'll* start to cry, and then you'll feel really, really bad about upsetting me." She'd rather go to his stupid-ass father and get the truth from him. Maybe toss in a Molly electric-shock by mistake too.

Devon looked up with a start, and for the first time all night, a faint smile played around his lips. Then the smile disappeared and he straightened up with a sigh. "He says that he knows all about our relationship, and not only does he not condone it, but he'll do everything in his power to shut it down. No matter how strongly I feel about you." Devon's voice had gone supernaturally soft and he kept his eyes fixed on the carpet as he continued on in a dull monotone.

"He wouldn't!" Rae couldn't believe it. "Can't he see that you're happy? Like really, truly happy?"

"He says despite everything I've done in school and for the PC, he's not remotely proud anymore. He says I've disgraced the family." He gave a brittle laugh. "In fact, he wants to flat-out disown me. Only the dickhead can't come up with a plausible reason since my mother doesn't know anything about tatùs or the rules that govern us."

Rae felt like her heart was breaking. As much as she loved Devon, this was never what she wanted, to put him at odds with his family, to turn his entire life upside-down. She would move heaven and earth to be with him, but not if that came at the price of his well-being. More than anything, his happiness was the thing she wanted most in this world.

"Devon," she cleared her throat softly as her voice broke, "maybe we should—"

"No," he cut her off firmly. "I know exactly what you're going to say, and it's never going to happen. I'm committed to this. To you."

"But if it's going to tear apart—"

"You know I'm off probation?" he asked suddenly.

"What?" Rae frowned in shock, thrown off her game. "You, but not me?"

Devon shook his head with a flat grin. "They probably just don't want you to fail your finals. But yeah, as of last week, they said I was ready to go back into the field."

A sudden weight in Rae's stomach seemed to anchor her to the bed. Of course he was. It was going to be exactly like last time. Him always gone, her never knowing where he was, if he was even all right. "So," she tried not to sound as glum as she felt, "when're you leaving?"

"I'm not."

"What?" Rae shook her head in confusion. "What do you mean?"

"I told them no," he said simply. "I refuse to go into the field without you."

"But you can work with Julian! He's fully capable—"

"We both know he's not right now," he cut her off. "But that's not the point. I'm taking a leave of absence until you're ready to go back out with me." He leaned forward and took her hand. "Don't you see, Rae? I'm making *this* my top priority, what we're doing right here. I never want you to doubt my priorities again. I want to have a life with you. Not a long distance relationship. A *life*."

Her eyes welled up with tears and he pulled her against his chest, chuckling. "See, I've made you cry anyway. I should just stop trying to avoid it."

She giggled and looked up at him with a watery smile. "I want to have a life with you too. I keep thinking about how much easier everything's going to be once I graduate. When we're both living in the city."

Devon's dimples flashed with his smile. "No more sneaking around. No more curfews. I can stay the night without having to worry someone will see..."

Rae's eyebrows shot up and she leaned back suggestively atop her bed. "Well, I'll let you in on a little secret, Devon. If you don't mind sneaking out...you can always stay over tonight..."

"Is that so?"

He leaned over her and lowered his lips down to her neck. "Why Miss Kerrigan, are you trying to seduce me?"

She shrugged coyly. "Actually, no. Sometimes it just seems to happen on its own."

He chuckled and began trailing feather light kisses up and down her jaw. "Can't argue with that. You sure you don't need to study?"

She laughed breathlessly. "Are you serious right now? It's after midnight!"

He smiled against her skin. "What can I say? I want you to be responsible." He slipped off his shirt and began fiddling with the fabric on hers, inching it higher and higher. "I don't want to distract you..." he teased.

Her eyes closed and she pressed her head back into the pillow. "Devon?"

"Yeah, babe?"

"Stop talking."

Before sunrise Devon snuck out her window, waving at her as he dropped soundlessly to the ground below. She watched him race across the grass and wondered why his father hated her so much. Had she not proven to him time and time again that she was not her father?

Unable to sleep, Rae dressed and made her regular trek to the library. She pushed open the heavy double doors, expecting to find everyone crunching for finals, which were just two days away, but instead, everyone was gathered around the main table, staring down at something in the center.

"What's going on?" Rae asked, worming her way to the front.

Rob flashed her a grin. "Just a little well-deserved R&R."

She gazed down at the table only to see a hundred pictures of her and her friends staring back up at her. It was an extensive collection of their time at Guilder; from photographs, to movie stubs, even to a few wrinkled first-year predictions as to what their tatùs would be.

"Whoa Maria," Andy said with a grin, "you look so much younger!"

Maria set down a crumbled diner receipt and grinned. "I do? Look at you! You're like a little baby! Look at those curls!"

Molly turned to Rae with a bright smile. "Do you remember when this was taken?" She held up a picture of her and Rae standing next to Riley's car. He had just gotten it and was being rather insufferable about the whole thing. While Molly was smiling politely, Rae looked like she'd been dragged into the picture by her fingernails.

"Oh wow!" She laughed. "Yeah I do!" She shook her head with a grin. "I was *so happy* when he graduated."

"I wasn't," Haley said suddenly.

The people around the table looked up with a start and Molly's jaw dropped. "You mean, you actually liked..."

Haley shrugged with an uncharacteristically playful grin. "He was hot. So, kill me."

The group erupted in laughter, and for the next couple hours, the textbooks were put away and they spent the time happily reminiscing about the last few years. When they finished discussing the past, they turned their talks to the future. Rae was right. Most all of them had gotten some sort of 'tatù government' job and were staying in the area. Actually, most all of them were living within a ten-minute radius of her and Molly's new apartment.

After, Rae and Molly walked slowly back across the grass, reveling in the nostalgia. Despite whatever madness Guilder had thrown their way, it had still been home for the last few years. No matter which way you looked at it, no matter the sometimes-questionable cost, their lives had most definitely changed for the better.

There was one thing that bothered Rae. Nothing horrible, just a weird little feeling that started tugging away at her stomach. Everyone in the pictures looked so much younger than they did now—Molly, Haley, Andy, Nic... None of them looked at all like how they did today.

None of them except Rae.

She'd looked at a dozen pictures. Held them up for comparison a dozen times. There was no denying it. She looked exactly the same now as when she started at Guilder. A little tougher, perhaps. A little more confident and mature. But physically...exactly the same.

She broke off from Molly with a wave and decided to head to Devon's room at Joist Hall to ask him if he'd ever noticed it as well. But her thoughts were instantly derailed the second she got upstairs. There was a huge wooden X where Devon's door was supposed to be. And when she peered inside, the room was completely empty.

"What the?" She turned in surprise as Devon and Julian joined her on the landing, both staring at the room in identical shock.

Devon's mouth fell open in bewilderment and he took a step forward. "Did you...did you do this?" he asked Rae.

She shook her head.

"Is this a prank?" he asked Julian.

Rae swallowed, Ellie's tatù giving her an indication of what had happened. She pushed the thought away, not believing it was right. She just had the thought, it wasn't tatù driven. "I just got here a second ago from the library. I was about to call you—"

"Well, clearly there's no need."

The three teenagers looked up to see the Dean walking slowly towards them.

"Dad?" Devon glared at him. "What the hell's going on?"

"Sorry, Devon." The Dean glared back at his son. "I found no other way to make myself clear." He crossed his arms over his chest, disgust clear on his face as he looked at Rae and Devon. "You've been officially evicted. You no longer have a home at Guilder."

Julian and Rae looked on in shock, but Devon took an angry step forward. "Is that really how you're going to play it? You're actually kicking me out? How freakin' old are you?" He stepped toward the room but his father blocked him. "Where the hell's all my stuff?!"

"Your things have been placed outside the Guilder gates," the Dean replied stiffly. "You can collect them as you leave. Or not. It's not my problem."

Devon's eyes flashed dangerously. "If you think for one second I'm just going to—"

Julian stepped neatly in between. "Devon can stay with me." Like Molly and Rae, he and Devon lived just across the hall. Julian spoke calmly, but he leveled the Dean with almost lethal-looking eyes. "Surely you don't have a reason to kick me out of Guilder."

"Or he can stay with me." Rae matched his glare. "Surely the golden son who has fallen from your good graces won't be homeless. You want an excuse to kick me out too?" She crossed her arms over her chest. "I just gave you one."

The Dean looked ready to explode.

Devon snickered. "I can just imagine what Headmaster Carter's going to say. Or how the Privy Council's going to react when they hear Kerrigan's been kicked out."

The Dean glared at all of them before he finally shook his head. "Fine! The *boy* can stay with Julian." He stomped angrily down the hall, muttering something about a staff meeting to save face.

Julian stared after him for a moment, before clapping Devon on the shoulder. "I'm going to go get your stuff. Here's my room key." He tossed Devon the key and then headed down the same stairs as the Dean, leaving Devon and Rae alone on the landing.

Rae watched Devon carefully, unsure what she should say, but he was in his own world, staring at the empty room like he couldn't believe his eyes.

"Come on, Dev," she said gently after a moment. "Let's go to Julian's room. Or better yet, let's go help him. Heaven forbid he has a vision while carrying your stuff."

Devon didn't budge. He just stared into the room. "I can't believe it," he muttered, wide-eyed and lost. "My own father? I just can't believe it..."

Chapter 12

The dreaded day had come and past. The notorious Guilder finals were finally over. Truly, finally, over. She was done with school. No need for A-levels, or college courses. Everything she would need from here on out would be taught at the PC training facility.

Rae could honestly say the exams were exactly as hard as she'd expected, maybe harder. At seven a.m. sharp, she and her friends trotted across the lawn to the cafeteria where they spent the next six hours slaving away over a test booklet the size of a small tree. As it turned out, each of her friends had their own way of coping with the stress. Halfway through, Molly had to ask for a new calculator because she'd fried hers with a jolt of nervous electricity. Haley's hair kept blowing around her with a self-made gust as though she was sitting outside, and poor Rob—whose ability to shift into an eagle was one of Rae's favorites—kept molting feathers.

But despite the difficulty, Rae set down the test booklet thinking that she had done just fine. Over the last few days, she'd finally started to get a handle on Ellie's tatù—and the extra boost had come just in time. With the exception of a few absurdly outlandish questions (advanced thermo-dynamics, anyone?), she'd been able to summon most every subject to memory. She'd found the essay portion of the exam particularly amusing.

'Pick one historical figure from Guilder's formation and explain how said person's contributions have affected you today.'

She wondered if Carter had a hand in picking the question. Perhaps more importantly, she wondered if he would be the one to grade her answer. She doubted her sarcastic prose and cheeky responses would make much sense to anyone else.

So, it was with a sense of great relief that she pried Molly away from her desk—surrounded by a graveyard of burnt pencil tips—and joined the rest of their class as they walked out into the sun. Now that they'd completed the written part of their testing, the only thing left was the practical application portion of the exams. And *that* was something that everyone was looking forward to.

They were to meet in the Oratory, one by one, for some sort of tatù demonstration. The details had been sparse, and when Rae asked Devon about it, he was rather fuzzy on the specifics himself. All he'd said was that it wasn't something she should be at all worried about, in fact, he knew personally she would rather enjoy it.

It was with this sense of jittery anticipation that she waited outside the Oratory with the rest of her peers. They'd been lined up alphabetically, but the second she'd found her place behind Rob, she'd been pulled out by a teaching attendant who simply said, "You go last."

"Great," she turned to Molly doubtfully, "they're going to crucify the infamous Kerrigan after all. Graduation antics and sweet revenge for all the trouble I've caused."

"Oh yes," Molly said practically, smoothing down her skirt, "we've all been planning it for months. I'm to bring the kindling."

Rae snorted and gave her friend a shove as she was called into the room. Everyone exited from the far door, so she hadn't been able to grill anyone on what was going to happen. And before she had the sense to switch into Julian's tatù and simply look ahead, her name was called.

"Kerrigan, Rae."

She shot the attendant a look as he barked it out. They were the only two people left standing outside and she looked around comically before turning back to him.

"Really? 'Kerrigan-dash-Rae?' You see a lot of other Kerrigans out here?"

He rolled his eyes with a long-suffering weariness. "Just get inside, Rae."

She saluted with a grin. "Yes, sir."

"And try not to hurt anyone..."

She heard him say it as she stepped inside, but before she could ask what he meant, the door shut behind her with a loud click. There was something abruptly startling about the sudden silence that followed. Rae didn't think she'd ever heard the Oratory so quiet. It was meant to be a noisy place. Full of laughter and strong echoes. As her eyes quickly adjusted to the dim lighting with the help of a certain fennec fox tatù, she took another step. Then, all at once, the lights flashed on and it took a moment to readjust her vision, but what she saw, for the first time, was what she was up against.

"Wow..." She couldn't help but laugh. "You've got to be kidding me."

Almost every seat in the house was full. Folding chairs had even been pulled out in front of bleachers, giving the huge room almost an arena feel. All the lights were pointed at the circled space in the middle. And there, standing at the center of it all, was Devon.

Rae caught his eye from across the room and he smiled. "Sorry. I couldn't tell you more," his soft voice was echoed off the domed ceiling and came back to the audience tenfold. There was a titter through the crowd as Rae walked out to meet him. "You did mention Guilder was a bit sketchy on the details."

"This is my demonstration?" she asked incredulously, gazing out at all the familiar faces.

As it turned out, the rest of her peers weren't dismissed when they were finished. Instead, they were sitting amongst the rest of the students and teachers. Even a few alumni had arrived early for the graduation banquet just so they could watch.

Watch the nefarious Kerrigan at work, Rae realized with a sudden chill.

Devon's eyes kept it light, inviting her to ask the questions she so badly needed to know.

Keeping a casual grin fixed on her face, she summoned Maria's tatù so she could speak to him telepathically.

Is there more to this than meets the eye?

He glanced up at the ceiling, then back down at Rae. A discreet nod to the affirmative.

How much more? Are there members of the PC here? People who want to know how 'dangerous' me and my tatùs really are?

"Not to worry, Rae," he teased lightly. The audience laughed, but only he and Rae knew what he was really talking about. "It's a Guilder tradition—everyone goes through it."

But they saved me for last.

Under the guise of stretching out his arms, he gave her a casual shrug.

Why?

"Must just be my lucky day they picked you to go last, and me to push the envelope," he continued, to the entertainment of the crowd. "Do me a favor, huh? Don't go easy on me." Their eyes met. "Show them what you're made of." Then, turning his back to the audience, he gave her a little wink.

A wide grin spread across Rae's face. They wanted a show? She'd give them a show.

The next second—she was gone.

There was a gasp from the audience and Devon spun around in dismay. "Invisible?" he called, shaking his head. "Really? Too scared to face me head on?"

A sweeping kick knocked his legs out from under him and he fell to the ground with a startled gasp. A second later, Rae shimmered into the air above him. "Aw Dev..." She leaned down. "I thought you knew me better than that."

There was a shriek of applause from the audience as the two of them spun around to face each other. Friends and strangers cheered. Rae didn't miss the money being exchanged as bets were placed. Only Devon and Rae's closest friends, sitting in the front row, refused to gamble. They happened to know them a bit too well to side against either one of them.

Devon pulled off his jacket and grinned, tossing it to the side of the floor. With a wicked grin, he started circling her, taunting her with a "come-hither", using his fingers to beckon her to fight.

Rae bit her lip to restrain a smile. It wasn't unlike the things he'd done just the night before.

"All right Rae, let's have it." He beckoned her forward. "Show them what you learned."

She cocked her hip to the side as she pretended to think about it. "Hmm...so many to choose from. Maybe a little of this?" A crackling stream of electricity sent him leaping backwards.

Devon touched his head, trying to smooth down his sudden static-ridden hair.

"Or maybe...we'd like a little privacy." In a flash, two rivers of fire poured from her hands, circling both of them before evaporating as quickly as they'd appeared.

There was a sudden hush from the crowd, a few of them even looked a bit nervous. In the front row, Rae's friends simply pulled up their shoes to avoid the flames, looking almost bored.

Then suddenly, there was a shout. "Use my tatù, Rae!"

Both she and Devon looked up into the crowd. It was a girl in her third year. One who could make her skin as hard and smooth as metal. With an answering smile, Rae held up her arms and watched as the silvery substance coated her entire body.

Standing just two feet away, Devon winced almost imperceptibly.

You're going to want to duck, or this is really going to hurt.

She swung out with all her might, but Devon was no longer there. He'd jumped over her body and kicked her square in the back, sending her sprawling forward onto the floor. He ran towards her as she rolled to a stop, but before he could reach her, she was on her feet, using a handy leopard tatù to pick him up and send him flying into the wall.

He hit the mat with a muffled crunch and slid down, panting but grinning all the while.

"I told you," he murmured as the crowd erupted again, "don't take it easy on me."

Rae grinned. "You asked for it."

The next second, she was sprinting towards him as fast as she could. But rather than staying on the ground, she switched into Ethan's tatù—summoning things that she needed. One by one, brick stairs flew up in the air in front of her, vanishing the second she'd climbed one and reached the other. Devon watched in dismay and the crowd looked on in amazement as she literally ran up into the air—catapulting down when she was over Devon's head and felling him to the floor. There was another deafening roar and Rae could pick out Ethan's voice among the throng as she bent down to help Devon to his feet with a smile.

Only—again—Devon was no longer there.

Rae had literally blinked and missed him. There was a whisper of air, and the next second, she was on her back, staring up in surprise as he pinned her shoulders to the ground.

"Sorry honey." No one could hear him now with the level of noise in the room. "Do you need me to slow down? Give you a moment to catch your breath?"

"Actually, no," she grinned coquettishly up at him, "this is giving me the greatest flashbacks from last night." Turning her head ever so slightly, she couldn't help but throw the Dean a little wink as she got to her feet and dusted herself off. His face turned the color of a boiled lobster as he fumed in silence.

"Seriously though," Devon cocked his head to the side, "even footing. My ink versus your, which is my, ink. What have you got, Kerrigan?"

Rae's body switched back to the fennec fox tatù with a familiar hum. "Let's see, shall we?"

What happened next was a blur of colors and sounds. Things were moving too fast for the crowd to see the details, but every now and then, someone would get thrown to the side, or launch down from the ceiling and they would cheer once more.

Even with her superior reflexes, Rae had to admit, it was taking everything she had to keep up with Devon. Without the benefit of her extra powers, when they were just regular fighting one-on-one, he was a force to be reckoned with. She'd turn one way—he'd feint another. She'd block his attack—he'd have one more right up his sleeve.

Fortunately, she'd had a brilliant teacher. And she had a few tricks up her sleeve as well...

In a tangle of limbs, Devon was suddenly on the floor. He looked up at Rae straddling him and blinked slowly before his lips curled up in an appreciative grin. "All right Kerrigan, you got me."

The explosion that followed almost took out Rae's eardrums. She helped Devon up and waved at the screaming crowd before stepping behind him self-consciously. She instantly switched out of his tatù so she wouldn't hear them full blast. In fact, she wished she could switch on Cassidy's and once again turn invisible, but she didn't think that would send the right message. She had just gotten a few more disbelievers on her side. Now was not the time to lose them.

She smiled politely as Carter stepped forward and formally dismissed them. The practical part of the exam was over. Finals were officially complete. There was another grand cheer following this pronouncement and the horde got to their feet, filing noisily out of the building to get ready for the graduation ceremony.

Rae saw her mother in the crowd and grinned as Beth made a beeline for her. "That was quite the show you put on, honey."

She hugged Rae tight, winding a hand behind her neck as she whispered in her ear, "And we both know, it's not even half of what you can do."

Rae pulled away, blushing. "Yeah, well, you know. No need to make *everyone* jealous. It was enough just to kick Devon's ass." She punched him good-naturedly and he shook his head.

"Doesn't matter. I was technically your mentor. So, whenever you win, everyone knows it's thanks to *my* teaching."

Rae's eyebrows shot up as she laughed. "Really? Is that how you're going to play this off?"

Beth chuckled and shook her head. "Speaking of mentoring, I think some kids want to talk to you." She cocked her head behind her at the gathered group of first years still waiting on the wings. "I'll let you guys get to it. But Rae, I want you to stop by my cottage before you head out for dinner tonight. I have a graduation gift to give you."

"I will." She kissed her mom on the cheek and waved the first years forward as Beth disappeared out the door. "All right minions, what do you have for me?"

"Well, it's actually a presentation," Ellie said importantly.

Rae chuckled as Julian and Molly joined them in the center of the floor. "Hey Julian, I thought you had a date today?"

He blushed. "Apparently something came up."

Devon laughed. "She stood you up, mate?"

"Shut up," Julian muttered.

Ellie cleared her throat. "We'd like to do our presentation."

"Now?" Molly asked in dismay. "Rae, we're going to need some serious time to get ready for tonight. I don't know about you, but I'm hoping my date's going to end really, really well if you know what I—"

Julian cleared his throat loudly and glanced at the kids.

Molly followed his gaze with a sigh. "Fine. But make it quick, kids. Clear and concise gets an A."

"Molls..." Rae smacked her arm.

"What? Like there's anything they've discovered that we haven't already been over with them anyway?" she said under her breath. Then she raised her voice a bit louder. "Except for Noah, of course. He gets an automatic A."

Rae rolled her eyes and motioned Ellie forward. "What do you have, Ellie. Dazzle us."

The tiny girl launched into a rather gripping tale, considering how boring most of the subject matter was.

She began to pace and narrate, as if reading their paper but not actually looking at it. "To the outside world, Cromfield lived a normal life. At least, as normal a life as he could whilst serving the King. He had been tasked with creating Guilder as a safe-haven for people with powers in the hopes that one of these people could help the King have a son. While none of them had that particular ability, the school remained long after both men were dead," Ellie paused dramatically before continuing, "at least, both of them were thought to be dead, transforming into the academy they all knew it as today." Ellie summed it up nicely— giving the broad strokes version of the paper in her hand. She covered the places he went, people he saw, and laws he put into action. She wound up the grand speech with the last place he was seen.

"And that was it," she concluded. "He was spotted leaving St. Stephen's Church after a midnight mass sometime early in the New Year. Although no body was ever found, he was officially presumed dead two years later. So, that's it. That's Jonathon Cromfield."

She turned to Rae proudly, but Rae was frozen in place—her mouth fell open and she was staring at the girl without blinking, lost in her own little trance. Molly nudged her with a frown, but when Rae didn't move, she snatched the paper from Ellie's hands with a sweet smile.

Devon stepped forward, giving Rae a 'what's up' look. "That's very good, guys. We can see a lot of effort went into this. You all pass with flying colors and our thanks. Now go! Run along!"

The children dismissed themselves and hurried out into the sun, as thrilled as everyone else that the school year had come to a close. Four friends remained in the Oratory, three of them staring at Rae as though she'd become slightly unhinged.

"Uh, Rae? Earth to Rae?" Molly shook her again. "Geez Devon, you must have knocked her down harder than you thought."

"SSC!" Rae gasped.

The other three exchanged a look before turning to her curiously.

"What're you talking about, Rae?" Devon asked with concern.

She turned to him with a look of open triumph. She couldn't believe they hadn't clued into this sooner. How in the world had they missed it? "The last place Cromfield was seen coming out of alive. St. Stephen's Church."

Devon nodded slowly. "Yes, that's what the first years said."

"*SSC*. Saint. Stephen's. Church." She punctuated each word.

There was a collective gasp as all four of them stared around their little circle.

"It's been under our noses the whole time," Julian muttered, taking the written report.

"That doesn't matter," Rae said firmly, "all that matters is we have a target now. We have a place to start looking."

Molly's eyes closed with a momentary grimace. "And it's certainly true to our luck..."

"What do you mean?" Devon asked with a frown.

"It's just typical." Molly shook her head. "The night of our big graduation, and how are we going to spend it? Breaking into a church..."

Chapter 13

"Well...it was fun while it lasted." Molly dropped her sweater on the floor in Rae's room before sweeping her red locks up into a tight ponytail.

"Sure was." Rae moved with a lot more enthusiasm, flipping through her closet at a breakneck pace. Instead of pulling out the long garment bag that beckoned invitingly, she reached beside it for a heavy black jacket.

"Wait—what was fun?" Devon asked with a frown. He and Julian were the only two who had not sprung into immediate action. Instead, they were watching the girls with twin looks of puzzlement splashed across their handsome faces.

Molly sighed, wiping off her lipstick with a tissue. "School, graduation. Well, the *illusion* of graduation." She glanced wistfully into the mirror. "Those precious seconds where I thought I might actually get to go out on my date."

"Wait, wait—hold up!" Devon demanded, crossing to the middle of the room to halt the action. "What're you talking about? Why are you not going out on your date? Wait a sec! Who are you suddenly dating?"

"Luke," Molly said innocently. "Rae didn't tell you?"

Devon's mouth fell open but he looked undeniably pleased. "No, she did not. That's awesome Molls!" His smile faded. "But...why are you not going?"

Rae smiled cheerfully. "Because we're breaking into a church."

Julian chuckled and took a seat on the bed. "Oh, this is going to be good."

Devon drew himself up to his full height. "There is to be absolutely no church breaking until after graduation. Do I make myself clear?"

Molly snorted in muffled laughter. "Okay, *Carter*. Actually, no, you don't."

"Rae, come on," Devon continued. "The two of you deserve to get all dressed up and walk across that stage. The church has clearly been there for hundreds of years, it's not going anywhere. The reservation I made downtown, however, expires at ten."

Rae just shook her head, pulling a long-sleeve shirt over her camisole. "Nope, we have our destination. We're going now. There's no telling what Cromfield is up to or what timetable he's working on. We've got to find him. Everything depends on it."

"*Everything* can wait a few hours." Devon pulled her to a gentle stop. "Rae, listen to me. You don't want to miss your graduation, trust me. There's something to be said for ending your old life before you move on with your new."

She faltered for a second and he pressed his luck.

"The church will still be there in a few hours, we can go right after the ceremony. But you and Molly have been working too hard for this. You need to walk across that stage."

Rae glanced at Molly, who was staring longingly at the garment bag.

Devon brought his lips to her ear and whispered softly, "End this chapter. Do it right. Then we can go see whatever the future has in store. Together."

Rae bit her lip and stared up into his eyes. "We can go right after the ceremony?"

He chuckled, kissing the tip of her nose before releasing her. "Right after the ceremony."

Julian shook his head. "You are hands down the strangest girl I've ever met."

Rae whirled around, a sarcastic reply on the tip of her tongue, but Molly silenced her with a feral shriek as she practically shoved the boys out of the room. "No time! If we're really going to do this, then we already lost four minutes arguing about it! We've got to move!"

Devon grinned as he jogged out the door. "See you at six, Rae." His eyes flickered inside to where Molly was working herself up into a crackling whirlwind of energy. "Good luck!"

The door closed silently behind him and Rae turned to Molly with a wary eye. "I'm not going to need to find you a sedative, am I?"

Much to her surprise, Molly leapt upon her, throwing her tiny arms around Rae's neck. Rae patted her gently on the back, both shocked and amused.

"What's this?" she asked tentatively.

Molly shuddered with a silent sob. "I'm just..." She pulled away and wiped a stream of sudden tears from her face. "I'm just so happy we get to wear these dresses!"

Rae's big speech about once-in-a-lifetime moments, how it was important to take a second to breathe and how it was okay to cry, vanished in an instant as she took a step back and surveyed her over-emotional friend.

"The dresses? Really?"

Molly stopped crying in an instant as her face lit up with glee. "Wait until you see them!"

What started out as a two-person beautifying extravaganza, quickly expanded as the door pushed open and two or three other girls from their graduating class pushed their way inside.

"Sorry to just drop in," Maria apologized, "but we were actually hoping that Molly could help do our hair...?"

Molly scoffed impatiently, but beamed to herself as she waved them inside. "All right, all right, I'll see what I can do. You guys are lucky I'm such an excellent multi-tasker. Haley! Plug in that straightener. Maria! Find me curling irons in three different sizes. Rae! Hairspray. Lots and lots of it." She shook her head despairingly. "Honestly...what would you people do without me?"

Three hours later, the tiny room had transformed into some sort of Barbie playhouse. Loud music blared from Rae's computer, pieces of popcorn and licorice scattered the floor, and the girls themselves? Well, the girls had been sculpted to perfection.

No longer did they look like the innocent little teenagers who had first started at Guilder all those years ago. They were going to cross the stage as elegant young women, ready to take their place in the world.

Molly did a phenomenal job, styling each girl to play on their strengths. Haley wore a statuesque white gown, which brought out her full height, while her hair was piled gracefully atop her head in a crown of regal curls. Maria, on the other hand, had gone for a sleek, modern look. Her jet-black dress was offset nicely by the new angular cut to her hair and dark red lipstick. Alecia, the resident doctor, was wearing a light pink baby doll that added a youth and softness to her often-serious face. While Molly had gone for a shimmering number in deep emerald green. It matched her eyes exactly and made her flaming crimson locks even more vibrant.

Rae slipped into the bathroom to change.

Molly was just setting in the final pin to secure locks to her head as she called for Rae. "Come on Rae! Out of the bathroom. I want to see how it looks."

There was a brief pause followed by a rustle of fabric.

"I...don't know about this one, Molls. It's a little extreme. Even for me." She stared at herself in the mirror. She should have known better than to leave Molly in charge of this.

Molly spat out the remaining bobby pins and turned her head sharply towards the closed door. "Have I ever steered you wrong?! Even once?! Come on! Get out of there!"

"Fine, but if this goes sideways, you're paying for my therapy..."

The door opened and Rae stepped out in her dress, fidgeting nervously as she waited for her best friend's opinion. Molly's eyes welled with automatic tears and she clasped her hands to her mouth. "Oh my gosh, Rae! Seriously. There are not words..."

"Really?" Rae asked anxiously, and she turned to the mirror in the room.

The dress was ruby red; a waterfall of tightly fitted silk that looped once over her shoulders before spilling all the way to the floor. Two sparkling silver shoes peeked out from just below, but with the way the silhouette was cut, Rae hardly needed the shoes to give her added height. It was elegant but undeniably sexy all at the same time. Elongating her entire body and offsetting her pale white skin, making it almost seem to glow in comparison. The bodice was a little on the lower side while still being modest, but when she turned around, the dress had absolutely no back. The graceful sweep of the fabric started up again just at the lower tip of her spine, placing her shimmering fairy tatù in full breathtaking view.

As for her styling, Molly had loosely curled the dark locks and let them spill naturally down her back. There were no pins, no hairspray—nothing except a fresh, tumbling wave of raven black. Makeup was also kept to a minimum. Rae wore no powder or foundation. She didn't need to. All she had was a touch of shimmer above the eyes offset with heavy dark mascara. That, and a vibrant blood-red lip, completed the look.

"You are...my masterpiece." Molly flashed a picture with her phone and tucked it away in her purse for safe keeping. "Seriously. I wish I could enter you in some kind of styling show." She frowned thoughtfully, considering this, as Rae rolled her eyes and made her way through the room.

The rest of the girls were gathering up their things to head downstairs and meet their dates. But before Rae could text Devon, she had to stop by and see her mother.

Molly, she called telepathically across the room. Molly's head shot up and she met Rae's eyes curiously amidst the noisy clutter. *Thank you for this. Really. This is going to be a perfect night.*

Molly's eyes misted over, but she said nothing to alert the other girls to their private conversation. She just pressed two fingers to her lips in a silent blown kiss, and smiled as she gathered up the rest of her equipment into a bag.

Still smiling, Rae swept down the stairs. Heads turned as she passed them in the halls, but for the first time, it wasn't out of curiosity or fear. It wasn't because she was Rae *Kerrigan*, the girl with two tatùs, and everybody wanted to get a look at the freak. All she saw in their eyes was a breathless sort of admiration. Their eyes widened and lingered appreciatively as she breezed past them. A few of the boys even whistled under their breath.

That was all well and good, she thought. But let's wait and see what my mother has to say about this risqué number. As it turned out, she needn't have worried.

"Oh my goodness!" Beth murmured as she opened the door to let Rae inside. "Honey, you just look..."

Rae's automatic smile slid off her face in horror as her mother burst into tears. "Oh, Mom," she patted her on the back and shut the door with her foot, "don't cry, come on. It's just graduation."

"But I'm here to see it," Beth whispered, taking Rae's hands. "A few months ago, I didn't even know I had a daughter. There was just this hole in my life, a constant wanting I couldn't explain." She wiped her eyes. "I would have missed this. This day would have come and passed and I would never have known." She gave Rae's wrists a little squeeze. "Except that you found me."

Rae's own eyes streamed over and Beth was quick to wipe them with a ready tissue. "Oh no, don't you dare. I haven't known her long, but I know that little best friend of yours well enough to know that she'll shock me into high heaven if I let you ruin your makeup before the ceremony."

Rae laughed and dabbed her face dry. "She does seem even more keyed up than usual..."

"So, how about it?" Beth asked with a smile. "Are you and Devon ready for your big date?"

"I think so." Rae was suddenly nervous. "He's taking me to Clos-Clos—something?"

"Clos Maggiore?" Beth nodded her approval. "I'm impressed. He's really pulling out all the stops for you."

Rae pawed the ground anxiously with her heel. "Well, I didn't realize it before, but we've never really had a *date*. Not a real one, anyway. I mean, we've gone out for missions before, and saved each other's lives before going out for food, but I'm not sure if that counts."

Beth's lips twitched, but she fought to keep a straight face. "I don't think it does. Well, here," she reached into a drawer on her desk and pulled out a small wrapped package, "I don't want to keep you."

Rae tore off the tissue wrapping with great suspense. She hadn't gotten a present from her mother since she was about four years old, and she had no idea what to expect. A little box tumbled out into her hands and she lifted the lid with a silent gasp. "Oh Mom! They're beautiful."

A pair of diamond earrings sparkled back at her. Only these weren't the little studs Rae would expect considering the stone. They hung down almost three inches, looping in an intricate design before ending in a little teardrop.

"They were your grandmother's." Beth took them out of the box and fastened them to Rae's ears as Rae held back her hair and watched in the mirror. "Passed down from generation to generation. Stories go, that your great-great-grandmother Liliana had to pawn them one Christmas to pay for presents. But her husband bought them back from the same man later that year."

Rae stared in awe at the dazzling effect as they sparkled against her dark hair. "Are they real? They can't be real..."

"They are." Beth smiled. "Probably cost as much as my first car, but every family's got to have heirlooms, right?" She stroked back Rae's hair with a look of tender pride. "Argyle brought them with him. He planned to give them to you at graduation but gave them back to me. They're yours now. Mother to daughter. One day, you can pass them on to your children."

Rae threw her arms around her mother's neck. "Thank you," she whispered. "They're absolutely lovely."

"So are you, my dear." Beth pulled away and gave her a once-over. "Now, go find that boy of yours. I'm sure he's pacing the halls."

Rae grinned and gave her a wave as she slipped out the door. "I'll see you at the ceremony."

A swarm of caterers were already setting up for the big event as she headed back across the lawns. They darted back and forth from the parking lot, carrying plates of appetizers, stacks of cutlery and stemware, and bags of ice. She wondered where they were all banished to once the actual ceremony began. She couldn't imagine that they would be allowed to stick around...heaven knows what they would hear.

'And the award for excellence in the field goes to Maria Morales, for her excellent use of telepathy when evading—'

"Rae?"

She looked up and saw Devon walking slowly towards her across the tall grass. The sight of him in a tuxedo momentarily took her breath away, and all she could manage in response was a small smile. But the look on his face had her puzzled. He was frowning as if he didn't quite recognize her and there was a question in his voice when he said her name.

All at once, her brain snapped into high alert.

The brainwashing device—it had to be. Either that or Kraigan had come back to campus and had momentarily stolen his tatù, rendering him temporarily disoriented. Of course, there was also the chance that another of their friends had been shot and Devon had donated all his blood.

"What is it?" she asked anxiously as she hurried towards him. She took his hand the next second, squeezing and searching his eyes. "What happened?"

He flashed his dimple and her heart cautiously slowed before speeding right back up. "You," he said simply. "You look..." His eyes clouded again and he shook his head with an incredulous grin. "How is it that we're dating?"

She blushed, as much from his compliment as from his inability to properly formulate one. "I'm just slumming it, I guess," she teased lightly. "Seeing what the other side has to offer."

He wound her arm gently through his, his eyes sweeping every inch of her body before coming to rest on her face. "Well, I'm very glad that you are," he said softly.

They smiled at each other for a long moment, gazing deep into each other's eyes, before all at once, he pulled abruptly away. "Okay then," he started speed-walking to his car, tugging her along behind him, "let's get going to the restaurant."

She stumbled slightly, giggling as she tried to keep up. "What's your hurry?" His face had turned abruptly solemn and the sight of it was cracking her up. "I'm in heels here, remember?"

He didn't slow his pace.

She finally tugged him to a stop. "Hey! Just a minute then." She leaned down to take off her shoes, sweeping her long hair off her shoulders, offering a view of her bare back. She glanced up, catching Devon's growl before he made it.

He groaned softly and looked pointedly away.

"What's your problem?" she asked with a little frown, lacing the straps of the stilettos around her wrist.

"Just...get into the car."

She did as she was told, and the next second, they were peeling away from the school. After a few minutes of silent driving, she chanced a peek at his face. "You want to tell me what's going on? Did you step on a nail or something?"

He shot her a look from the corner of his eye, his lips twitching up and betraying him with a grin. "I can't be held responsible for my actions...when you're wearing that dress."

"Oh." Rae looked down at the red silk in surprise before smiling to herself. "Ohhh!"

"I thought it was best we get to a public place as soon as possible. Otherwise, there's no telling what might happen." He stroked a finger from her thigh to her knee, feeling the fabric. "And I really don't want to accidently rip this before you walk across the stage."

Her face flamed as red as the dress and she turned her head to stare deliberately out the window. "Understood."

They got to the restaurant about twenty minutes later and slowed to a stop as a white-gloved valet stepped forward to take their car. Devon shot her an almost anxious smile as she gathered up her purse and gave her hair one last cursory check.

"Are you ready?" he asked softly.

It was right then, as his voice cracked a little at the end, that Rae realized he was just as nervous to be doing this as she was. Their first ever date. As she peered up at the tall columns beckoning them inside, she decided he couldn't have picked a more intimidating place to do it.

She tucked her hair reflexively behind her ears. "Ready if you are."

With that, the two of them strolled arm in arm up the marble stairs.

If Rae had thought the restaurant was intimidating on the outside, she couldn't believe how much worse it was once they breezed through the double doors. The second they were in, both of them pulled up short, arms tightening instinctively around each other as their eyes tried to adjust to the overwhelming sparkle of a million iridescent lights. It was beautiful, there was no denying it, but that beauty seemed to come at a dauntingly oppressive price. Everywhere they looked was gold. Gold plates, gold silverware, gold lining on the velvet tablecloths. And where there wasn't gold, there was crystal. The glasses, the vases, the chandeliers, the tops of the little canes the butlers carried as they showed them inside. Yes, butlers! With canes!

"This is fancier than the Royal Ball..." Rae muttered as they were shown to a candlelit table in the center of the floor. "Where did you find this place?"

Devon's eyes darted almost apologetically around. "I Googled 'top-rated restaurants in London'." He looked distinctly embarrassed. "I wanted to take you somewhere nice."

"It *is* nice," Rae was quick to reassure him, settling into her chair with a deliberately casual smile. "It's very nice. Nicer than nice."

"Madame et Monsieur," the waiter interrupted her. "Today we will be starting with either one of two dishes. Eggplant soufflé or camembert infused with honey and wheat grass."

He paused, clearly waiting for them to decide, and Devon caught Rae's eye across the table. A single eyebrow cocked on his handsome face. "Can you hold on a minute?" he asked the waiter.

Fifteen minutes later, they were happily munching on a bag of fish and chips, lying back on the roof of Devon's car. They'd made a little mat of old newspapers between them to catch the grease, and were quietly staring up at the stars, smiling with contentment.

"This," Rae took a slurp of her milkshake, "is more my speed."

Devon laughed and slipped his arm beneath her neck. "Mine, too. Sorry about before. I don't know what I was thinking."

"You were incredibly sweet!" She giggled at the absurdly awkward scene before returning her eyes to the sky. "And it was certainly memorable."

"I swear, if you'd said you wanted the eggplant, I would have stuck it out the whole time with you."

"I was terrified that *you* were going to say that. Then I'd have to sit there, pretending I spoke French!"

He rolled onto his side and gazed at her affectionately. "You do speak French, genius."

That's right, she did. Well, technically she could understand every language. It was an amazing tatù she'd picked up from the future Queen of England. "I forgot about that! Technically yes then, but I don't know any French foods," she countered. "Unless they were serving croissants. That and, well, the only other thing I know is that they like to eat frogs. And French fries."

"I would not have made you eat frogs on your graduation," he promised.

She rolled onto her side so she could see him as well. "Oh yeah, why not? You actually *fought* me on my graduation. What's a few frogs..."

He threw back his head and laughed. "Sorry I couldn't tell you beforehand. I didn't want to ruin the surprise."

"I know your dad wasn't very happy," Rae said tentatively. They had generally avoided the subject of Devon's father since he'd technically kicked him off school grounds the day before.

Devon sighed but shook his head with an honest shrug. "I can't help that. It's actually something I've come to realize—while sleeping on Julian's floor." He flashed her a dry grin. "I can't help how he feels any more than I can control my own heart. He'll come around in time—or he won't. I don't know. But there's nothing I can do to change it either way. I'm out now. It's time for me to start my own future. Free of the protective eye of my father."

Rae mulled this over, impressed as ever by his predictably mature response. "Today's my last day there too. As of tomorrow, Molly and I are free and clear to move into our new place."

Devon shut his eyes and rolled onto his back, tilting his face up to the stars. "You have no idea how amazing that sounds. I can't believe it's finally here. It seems like we've been waiting forever."

"It's here. I'm not staying back at Guilder to mentor like you did." She laughed. "Ironically, I was never asked."

Devon chuckled. "I kinda offered to do it. Carter agreed."

"Really?"

He shrugged. "Carter's not as tough as he looks. He pretends to not want us to be together but sometimes I get the feeling that he's trying to push us to be."

Rae reached for his hand and squeezed it. "He's got the hots for my mom. He's trying to make it less obvious by having a Kerrigan in the spotlight." She wadded a piece of newspaper with her free hand and tossed it perfectly into the bin by the car. "I don't care whatever the reasoning is. Come tomorrow, you and I can finally start on this 'life together' that you're always going on about."

He poked her in the ribs and she giggled. "As long as it doesn't include more dinner dates like this one—I'll be just fine."

He brushed the bag of food to the side and rolled on top of her, holding himself carefully over her body so as not to wrinkle her dress. "Whatever am I going to do with you?"

"Hmm... I can think of one or two things."

He was just leaning in to kiss her when a sudden alarm dinged on his phone.

She pulled away in surprise as he pulled it from his pocket and switched it off.

"Hold that thought," he grinned, "we have a graduation to get to."

She blinked in disappointment as he slid off the car. "You actually set an alarm?"

He rolled his eyes and offered her a hand. "Rae, please. I set the alarm the minute I saw you in that dress."

Rae had never seen the school so packed. Every slot was full in the car lot and they actually had to park on the winding side street that led up from the main gate. As they walked arm in arm into the main auditorium for the ceremony, Rae finally saw the families of the people she'd been going to school with all these years. Mothers with the same shade of hair, fathers with the same smile. It was surreal. Once you were at Guilder, it was kind of like the rest of the world faded away. It was easy to forget that it was even out there, that anything else existed outside the tiny bubble. But sure enough, the school year had come to a close and the walls of their little community had been lowered down temporarily to let the rest of the world come inside.

"Rae, Rae!"

She turned around to see Nicholas waving frantically, tugging along an older man with the exact same glasses as his son. "Hey Nic," she greeted him as they got closer.

"Rae, this is my dad, Thomas MacGyver. Dad, this is Rae."

"Rae Kerrigan," Mr. MacGyver said warmly, holding out his hand. There was no malice in the way he said her last name, it was spoken only as an introduction. "Nicholas has told me all about you." They shook with a smile. "I saw you in the Oratory today. I have to say, I'm very impressed."

"Oh," Rae blushed, "that was all Devon Wardell. He knows how to make me look good."

"I'm sure."

A bell tolled from inside and all of them looked on towards the auditorium.

"Well, we better get our seats," Nic said hastily. "I'll see you up there, Rae. Bye Devon."

The two of them rushed away as Rae and Devon proceeded slowly inside. All the normal chairs and testing equipment had been pushed aside, leaving a sea of finely decorated white circular tables, each seat with a corresponding place holder.

"Let's go see where we're at." Devon guided her swiftly through the crowd.

Every now and then, someone would brush up against her or she would inadvertently shake the hand of someone new. Each time, the warm buzz of an unfamiliar tatù would hum through her veins, warming her blood with the very thought of it. By the time they reached their table, she had a bit of a head rush.

"You okay?" Devon asked softly as they took their seats.

Rae's eyes were dilated in wonder. "I think I can melt that candle with my mind..."

He patted her sympathetically on the shoulder and glanced around. "Do me a favor? Don't."

She shot him a sarcastic smile as Molly and Luke suddenly sat down at the table beside them.

"Luke!" she said in surprise. "Great to see you! Having a good time?"

"Dinner was wonderful," Molly said dreamily as Luke and Devon shook hands. "We went to this place called Clos Maggiore. Have you heard of it?"

Rae bit back a smile. "Sure haven't." As Molly started babbling on to Devon, she turned to Luke with a conspiratorial whisper. "Did you go with the camembert or the soufflé?"

His lips parted in surprise, before they were suddenly joined by Rae's mother. Beth took one of two remaining seats on the opposite side of the table, and squeezed Rae's hand in greeting.

"Mom, there's someone I want you to meet." Rae gestured beside her. "This is Luke."

As Luke looked up, Beth's face paled. "Luke? The one who found me? The one who brought us together?"

Rae nodded.

The second she did, Beth bolted right back up from the table and pulled out Luke's chair, tugging him to his feet. He gasped in surprise, but before he could say anything, she was embracing him in a hug so hard it turned his hands blue.

"Thank you," she murmured softly when she finally released him. "You've no idea what you've given me. What you've given us. As long as I live, I can never repay you."

Luke blushed beet red and stammered his excuses. "It's really no big deal Ms. Kerrigan—"

"Please, call me Beth." She smiled at him fondly. "And it is a big deal. It's truly the greatest thing anyone's ever done for me. Please know you always have a seat at our table, a place in our home."

He smiled and sat down quickly, scooting closer to Molly, but looking very pleased with himself. Meanwhile, Devon leaned over and whispered to Beth, "What about me? You never gave me the 'seat at our table' speech."

Beth shook out her napkin matter-of-factly and placed it on her lap. "Luke's not the one sleeping with my daughter."

Perhaps it was well-timed that Carter chose that particular moment to take the only remaining seat. His eyes glanced over Luke curiously before coming to settle on Beth. "You look lovely tonight," he said softy. The tender look in his eyes made Rae's stomach turn and she kicked her mom under the table.

"Don't you need to be sitting with the rest of the faculty, sir?" Rae asked pointedly.

He rewarded her with a tight smile. "Actually, no. As headmaster of this school I can generally sit where I please."

Devon squeezed Rae's hand under the table and she lowered her voice so only he could hear. "Great...that's just great."

Just then, the lights dimmed and the room fell silent. An official-looking man Rae had never seen stood up to make a speech, then one by one, she and her classmates were called up to walk across the stage.

It was almost funny. After all this work, all these late night missions and life or death moments of truth, they were handed a small slip of paper signed by both Carter and Dean Wardell.

And that was it.

Rae walked back to her seat feeling rather deflated. A strange hollow feeling had settled in the pit of her stomach, a feeling she saw reflected in Molly's eyes as well.

"So, that's all?" Molly said, sounding a bit underwhelmed. "After all this?"

Devon chuckled under his breath. "I told you: graduation's a rite of passage, but the ceremony itself is pretty lame."

"I'll say." Rae held up her diploma to the light. "This looks like binder paper."

"I assure you it isn't, Miss Kerrigan," Carter snapped peevishly. "And the ceremony's not over yet." His eyes sparkled. "We still have our awards of achievement to hand out."

Both Rae and Molly sat up a little straighter as he walked to the stage to present them.

"Don't get your hopes up," Devon warned quietly.

"Oh, come on," Molly shot back. "No one has done more to help this school and keep it safe than me. And Rae, of course," she added hastily.

Rae rolled her eyes and turned her attention to the stage. Carter was holding two plaques in his hand: the awards for Excellence in the School, and Excellence in the Field. As he tapped the microphone, the room fell quiet again.

"This year, Guilder's awards for excellence were rather easy to place. When the faculty cast their votes, both names came up unanimous. So, let us begin." He held up the first plaque. "The Guilder award for Excellence in the School...goes to Nicholas MacGyver. Come up here, Nic."

Molly and Rae clapped politely along with the rest of the room. They supposed it made sense. Nic was undoubtedly the brightest one in their class. It made sense that he'd be getting the award for academia. He stumbled up to the stage, shook Carter's hand, and waved it in the air for a second before returning to his seat.

This time, the pressure was on. The entire graduating class sat on the edge of their seats as Carter cleared his throat to begin again. "And lastly, the Guilder award for Excellence in the Field. As many of you know, the Guilder Academy serves as a gateway of sorts, placing its students in various work programs as early as their junior year. We've had students go on to become lawyers, ambassadors, even members of parliament. This year, the student we've selected is a little different. While her gift made her the perfect fit for the field of choice, it's her commitment to excellence and passion for her work that has made her this year's recipient."

Rae could almost hear him calling her name. All the blood she spilled for this school, for the Privy Council. All the sweat and tears—the cover-ups and collusions. This was her moment. The chance to finally prove herself. And best of all, her mother would be here to see it.

"The Guilder award for Excellence in the Field goes to...Alecia Montgomery!"

"That was such bullocks!" Rob swore as the rest of the graduating class mingled politely as the party disbursed. "I mean, no offense Alecia, you do great work, but come on!"

Molly giggled, sipping her second champagne. "That's so freaking rude, Robbie."

Alecia held up her hand. "I was as surprised as the rest of you. That being said..." She held up the plaque and waved it around in their faces with an uncharacteristically childish grin. "Suck on that!"

The group cracked up as Devon pulled Rae a step back so he could whisper in her ear. "I warned you not to get your hopes up. It's a Catch-22. The agents for the Privy Council undoubtedly do more for anyone to keep our community safe. *However*, the school can't admit who's in the PC and who isn't. Because of that, the award always goes to someone with a regular job."

She pinched him hard in the side. "You could have told me that."

"And miss watching you get all worked up for nothing? Not a chance." He chuckled. "Plus, you have a cross of two tatùs, that's kind of like cheating."

She giggled and was about to say something equally cutting, when his eyes suddenly cooled and he took a step back. She followed his gaze over her head to where his father was cautiously approaching them through the crowd.

The second Devon saw him, he detached himself and started walking away. "I'll meet you back at your room, Rae. We can leave for that other thing whenever you're ready."

Rae hated the pain in his eyes. "Devon, wait—"

"Hey," he squeezed her hand as his eyes sparkled down into hers, "I'll see you soon."

Without another word, he turned and vanished through the crowd. Rae braced herself for what was sure to be an uncomfortable conversation with the Dean, but before he could reach her, a tiny bouncing girl stepped in between them.

"Rae! Congratulations on graduating! That's amazing!" She leapt upon Rae in a huge hug, oblivious to the Dean watching just a few steps behind. "I don't know what I'm going to do without you next year. I can't imagine finding a better mentor."

Rae shook her head with a smile. "That's crazy, Ellie, you've already got your ink down better than I do. You're going to do incredible things with it."

"But it's not just that." The little girl's eyes welled with tears. "You helped me with...well, a whole lot more this year."

She reached suddenly behind her and tugged forward a middle-aged man. He looked a lot like her, the same dusty hair, the same sprinkling of freckles. Before Rae knew what was happening, he reached out and shook her hand. A new ability coursed through her body, yet, it felt very similar to one she already had. Understanding. This had to be Ellie's father, where one half of her tatù came from.

"Mr. Bellings," she said automatically, "it's a pleasure to meet you."

He cupped a second hand over hers, refusing to let go. "The pleasure is all mine." He stared at her with wide, earnest eyes. "Ellie told me about everything you did for her this year," his voice dropped several decibels, "everything you did for our entire family. Miss Kerrigan, I really can't thank you enough. It's made all the difference. Ellie's mother and I...well, we thank you from the bottom of our hearts."

Rae's eyes teared up, but she held them back with a gracious smile. "It was my pleasure. Ellie's an amazing girl. Anything I can ever do to help—anytime—you just let me know."

"We might just take you up on that." His eyes twinkled as he led a euphoric Ellie away, inadvertently leaving no one standing between Rae and Dean Wardell.

She spun on her heel to make a hasty exit, but he caught her arm with a gentle hand.

"Miss Kerrigan?" It was the first time he didn't say her name with revulsion and disgust. "Do you mind if we...took a walk?"

Rae hesitated. Big time. Was it betraying Devon to talk to this monster? After a few seconds deliberation, she decided she might as well hear what he had to say, and she followed him outside.

"I know you don't think much of me," he began bluntly, leading her through the gardens.

She blinked in surprise. But if honesty was the name of the game, so be it. "I don't like how you don't think much of your son," she replied. She had more on the tip of her tongue to spout out but caught herself.

She was expecting a fight, but he simply bowed his head and nodded. "It certainly must seem that way, I suppose." Once they were a safe distance away, he pulled her to a stop. "Rae, let me be honest with you."

She shifted nervously. "Um...all right. You seem to have been pretty brutally honest since I met you."

"When I was a student at Guilder, I developed an infatuation...with your mother."

What the hell?! Did everyone have a crush on dear old mom?! Rae struggled to keep hold of her emotions and nodded calmly as he continued.

"Of course, she wasn't interested in me. She was interested in your father. When the two of them got married and all their trouble began, I took it as a strange consolation. I told myself: this was what happened when you mixed two tatùs." He shook his head in shame. "After the fire, when she was presumed dead, I, of course, felt terrible about my reaction. After all, I'd never meant it with any harm, it was only ever intended to shield my own feelings from rejection. But needless to say, I latched onto the law of our community with a vengeance. That mixing ink and producing hybrids was strictly forbidden—an abomination." He glanced up quickly, worried he'd offended her, but she kept her face free of emotion.

"It's how I raised Devon," he confessed. "Although my son has always been more open-minded and compassionate than me. I remember the first time I saw you two together. The undeniable attraction." He shook his head. "It felt like there was a storm inside of me. Not only had my son repeated my mistake and forsaken one of our most important laws, but he'd fallen for Beth's own daughter. I suppose, in a way, I thought that by keeping you two apart, I was protecting him somehow."

"You weren't," Rae said softly. "You were hurting him beyond belief."

The Dean bowed his head submissively, a deep sadness in his eyes. "I see that now. You see, my feelings for Beth were never as profound as Devon's are for you. How could they be? It was nothing more than a childhood crush. But you and Devon..." He sighed. "What you have is special. You are the best thing in his world—the thing that makes him the happiest. Whatever you may think of me, Miss Kerrigan, whatever judgments I may rightly deserve, know this: I value my son's happiness more highly than anything else."

There was a sudden pause in the conversation and Rae looked up at him cautiously. "Sir, what exactly are you saying?"

His eyes warmed and he reached out suddenly and extended his hand. "I'm giving you my blessing. If you still want it, that is."

Rae blinked in astonishment. Could this be happening? Could this be real? Or was this some kind of trick? She never felt like she could wholly trust anyone. She glanced down at his hand for a full five seconds before she reached out and shook it in her own. His ink was the same as Devon's, less developed and yet she could tell it was almost the same. "Thank you, sir, I...I appreciate that. I know Devon will too."

"I hope so," the Dean replied nervously, "I'm planning to speak to him tonight but it looks like he's gone. Maybe tomorrow, then?"

"He'll be thrilled." Rae smiled, desperate to see the look on Devon's face when he heard the news.

The Dean nodded briskly, obviously unaccustomed to so many emotions in just one night. "Well, in that case, you kids enjoy your evening. Congratulations again Rae, on graduating."

"Thank you, sir." She bid him goodnight with a wave and headed back up to her room, grinning from ear to ear. She'd woken up expecting to have a day full of surprises, but she certainly hadn't counted on this. She was still smiling happily to herself when she pushed open the door to her room and stopped short.

Devon, Molly, and Julian stood in front of her, decked out head to toe in black.

"What's this?" she asked, momentarily forgetting herself.

Julian grinned. "We have a church to get to."

Molly held out a matching jumpsuit. "Happy graduation."

Chapter 14

"So, what exactly are we supposed to be looking for?" Molly asked again as the four of them stomped across the lawn to the parking lot.

There were still a few stragglers dressed in their graduation finery, most students wouldn't be moving out until the following morning, but no one took any notice of their black spy gear as they crossed campus. When you went to a school like Guilder, you learned not to ask those sorts of questions.

"I don't know." Rae shook her head. "Anything—everything. Stuff that can link us to Cromfield. Something to tell us what he's up to or where he's going next."

"What if Cromfield's there in person?" Devon asked softly. "Have you thought about what we're going to do if that's the case?"

Rae glanced at Julian who shook his head with a frown.

"I don't see that happening."

It was a temporary condolence, but hardly a long-term fix. By now, all of them knew exactly how quickly the future could change. It was a house of cards, teetering with every slightest decision.

"I doubt he's even alive. It seems impossible." Molly huffed, "Okay, so what're we going to do if—"

"Hey! Where are you guys going? You're missing the after party!"

The four of them stopped in their tracks as Rob and Andy came barreling up, followed closely by a slightly inebriated-looking Haley. Both groups stopped and stared at each other for a moment, sizing each other up, before Devon cheerfully answered Rob's question.

"Oh, you know. Just off to save the world."

Andy and Rob clinked beer bottles before raising them Devon's way. "We salute you for that, we really do, man. So, you guys need any help?"

Andy hiccupped and Rae tried not to smile. "Actually, we got it this time, but thanks. We'll see you guys tomorrow morning, okay?"

"Right-o," Haley giggled loudly, pulling the boys along after her as they headed to rejoin the party.

Rae watched them leave for a moment before glancing at Molly. "You sad that we're not going to the after party?"

Molly's eyes narrowed in disapproval as she watched Haley tripping up the stairs. "Actually, no. Not in the slightest."

Rae grinned and grabbed her arm as they headed to the car. "Me neither."

When they got to the lot, Devon reached automatically for Julian's keys, but Julian held them up above his head, walking casually to the driver's side. "Not this time bro, but thanks."

Devon pulled up short, clearly uncomfortable with what he imagined would blow up into a full-blown confrontation. "Look man, we're going to have enough problems on this trip without—"

"You mean the cop that's going to try to pull us over on Hillhurst Drive? Or the fact that the seventh stair leading up to the sanctuary is cracked down the middle?"

The group looked up in astonishment and Julian stared into Devon's eyes. "I got it," he said simply.

Devon stared at him for a moment, still rather blown away, before nodding and sliding into the passenger's seat. "I believe you do. Good job, mate."

Molly scampered in behind him, and Julian gave Rae a wink before joining them as well.

The drive to the church was quiet and uneventful. Molly, the usual conversational hub, spent all her time texting. Rae figured it was to Luke. Julian carefully avoided driving anywhere near Hillhurst Drive. Rae and Devon silently held hands, wondering what was to come. When they finally pulled up in the deserted lot, they looked up at the abandoned church with more than a little trepidation.

"How're we going to get in?" Molly asked quietly as they walked to the back door.

"Don't worry about that." Rae held open her hand and the air shimmered above it. "All we need is a key." She inserted the newly created key and the lock clicked open with a reverberating boom they could hear echoed all throughout the sanctuary.

The kids looked around nervously before slipping inside, one by one. Rae worked Ethan's ink again and four flashlights appeared in their hands. The beams of light darted around this way and that, taking in the magnificence of the old cathedral six bright inches at a time.

"It's beautiful," Molly finally murmured.

Rae nodded as a strange emotion tightened her chest. "My parents got married here." The others turned to her in shock but she kept her eyes fixed on the pulpit. "Their marriage certificate was in that box I opened with Luke. Performed by a Father Amos. I wonder if he's still here?"

"Let's hope not," Julian said quietly. "Come on, let's split up and hurry. There are too many people in this part of the city for me to get a clear vision of what's going to happen."

He and Molly went one way, while Rae and Devon went another. Between the four of them, they had the bulk of the church searched in no time. There was simply nothing out of the ordinary. No hidden doors, no secret locks—no hint to point them to Cromfield. About thirty minutes after setting out, the four of them met back in the sanctuary.

"Nothing?" Molly asked with disappointment.

"Nothing," Devon replied. "We checked everywhere except the groundskeeper's shed, and I seriously doubt there's anything left out there in the elements."

Rae sat down abruptly on a pew. She couldn't find words to express her disappointment. After months of researching, months of trying to track this man down, this was literally the only lead that they had. If there was nothing here, she had no idea where to go next.

"What do you want to do, Rae?"

She rubbed her eyes and shook her head. "I don't know. I guess we'll just come back in the morning and try to talk to someone who works here. See if they remember seeing anyone that looks like Cromfield, or Jennifer, for that matter."

With heavy hearts, they headed to a hotel two streets over. Devon paid for the rooms in cash and the four of them bid each other a subdued goodnight before heading off to bed. But just a few minutes after Rae shut the door, there was a soft knock.

"Come in," she called quietly.

It opened and Devon walked inside. "You don't lock your hotel room door?" he asked accusingly. "I could have been anybody. You don't know."

She sat down on the bed with a careless shrug. "I'm pretty sure I could take anybody who was stupid enough to try to rob me in the middle of the night."

"I could have been Kraigan."

This made her pause. "I wonder if he's made any progress," she mused aloud. "You know, I don't even know if he'd tell me if he'd already found her. In his mind, it's not like he owes me anything."

Devon's eyes grew hard as he locked the door pointedly behind him. "To tell you the truth, I honestly don't care which one of them makes it out alive. Either way, I'm coming after the one who's left."

Rae considered this for a moment. "I agree, but..."

"But what?"

"I don't think I can be so quick to dismiss family."

Devon's jaw dropped open. "You have to be kidding me. He tried to *kill* you, Rae."

"But that's him, not me. He is my half-brother, after all, and I don't have much family left."

Devon was quiet for a long while before he muttered, "Family's overrated."

Rae glanced over at him before stifling a sudden smile. "We'll see."

He cocked his eyebrows sarcastically. "We'll see?"

She grinned. "I'll ask you again tomorrow."

He sat down on the mattress beside her. "What's that supposed to mean?"

"Nothing. It's not for me to say. You'll find out soon enough."

"Is that so?"

She shrieked and leapt away, but he caught her by the ankle and dragged her back, tickling her mercilessly until she begged for reprieve. They curled up under the blankets without another word, each lost in their own thoughts.

It wasn't until the clock struck midnight that Devon wound his arm around her shoulders. "I love you, Rae."

Her heart literally skipped a beat as she snuggled deeper back into his arms. She didn't think she'd ever get tired of hearing those words. "I love you, too."

They woke up at the crack of dawn and headed downstairs to see Molly and Julian already waiting for them at a café in the lobby. The only problem was, they weren't alone.

"Luke?" Rae asked incredulously.

"Hey guys," he greeted them nervously, downing his espresso in a single shot.

"What the hell is he doing here?" Devon asked directly. His eyes fell on Julian, but Julian merely shook his head and shrugged.

"Don't look at me. He was here when I came down this morning."

"Luke," Rae asked tensely, "what's going on? Why are you here?"

He held up his hands innocently. "I was invited."

All eyes turned to Molly.

"Oh, come on," she defended herself, "the guy went into a coma. It's his fight, too. Plus...I got him a beanie already."

Devon shook his head. "I swear Molls, this isn't—"

"Devon," her usually playful voice was suddenly serious, "it's his fight, too."

There was no denying that. Cromfield was everybody's problem.

Before anyone could say anything else, Rae held up her hands for peace. "She's right. He's coming. We're going to need all the help we can get."

A muscle in Devon's jaw twitched, but he said nothing.

Luke, on the other hand, was grinning from ear to ear. "Finally," he exclaimed, "I get to do some actual fieldwork—real spy stuff. Not just staying behind and manning the computers."

"That's fine, but if we run into any..." She glanced up at the approaching waitress and edited quickly. "Uh...tattooed trouble?" The table snickered as the waitress refilled their coffees and left.

"I know, I know! I heard it all last night," Luke finished her thought. "I'm to stand behind Molly and not move for any reason whatsoever."

Rae raised her eyebrows and looked at her friend, but Molly quickly buried her head in her cappuccino. It looked like someone's date had ended on a good note after all. Speaking of which, what had happened with Julian's date? Or whatever it was he had said... something about other plans? She'd have to ask him about that later. Maybe the girl he was interested in couldn't make it, or had broken things off.

They finished breakfast in a hurry and chose to walk the two city blocks back to the cathedral. They were in luck, the only cars in the parking lot appeared to belong to a priest and the groundskeeper. The last thing they needed was a stray member of the congregation coming in for some ill-timed counseling.

"Okay, so here's the deal," Rae muttered as the five of them walked inside, "we're going to pretend like we're students, okay? Just doing a research paper, trying to track down some old people and files. We're absolutely not going to use our real names. We're absolutely not—"

"Bethany?"

Rae jumped in her skin and spun around to find herself staring into the confounded eyes of a priest. He was staring back at her with equal astonishment, and with an urge she couldn't explain, she found herself speaking without thought.

"Father Amos?"

The father took a step forward. "Yes, but...it can't be you. You haven't aged a day."

A warm flush spread through Rae's chest as she walked down the aisle to meet him. "I'm not Bethany. I'm her daughter, Rae."

"Bethany and Simon had a daughter!" The priest threw up his hands in delight. "That's wonderful news. So, how are they doing then? Are they still living in London? I haven't seen them in years."

Rae edited with a careful smile. "My mother sends her love."

He smiled reminiscently. "She was the most beautiful bride I had ever seen."

Rae sat down on one of the pews and gestured him to join her. "So, you did marry them, then? Right here in this church?"

"Right here in this church," he echoed. "I'd always hoped to see Beth again, but I haven't heard from her since the big day. I saw your father, of course, but never your mother."

A chill ran up Rae's spine and she saw Devon shoot her a look. "You saw my father?"

"Yes, of course." The priest was talking freely now, delighted by the memories and the company. "He often came in here with another woman." His eyes clouded over. "I often worried. It was your mother's maid of honor, I think."

"Jennifer?"

"Yes, Jennifer! I always thought Jennifer and Simon were related. Cousins, perhaps? Delightful young woman. A real history buff."

Rae leaned back against the pew, trying desperately to stay casual. "What makes you say that?"

"Well, it's an ancient cathedral, it struck her fancy each time she was in," Father Amos explained. "She was especially interested in the catacombs beneath the foundations in the cemetery."

The catacombs beneath the cemetery?

Rae glanced behind her and her friends shared a tortured look.

Of course it had to be under the cemetery...

This time, instead of waiting for daybreak, the group waited for dark. The minute the moon came up from behind the trees, they hopped over the fence and ran to make their way into the cemetery. Their dark clothes blended in with the night, and they crouched beneath the ever-encroaching mist to hide themselves from the outside world as they came up with a plan.

"So, now what?" Molly hissed, glancing nervously at the crumbling headstones. "And please don't say start digging."

Rae shook her head. "They would have needed easier access. Maybe a tunnel going in through one of the mausoleums? Julian, can you see which one?"

He glanced around the darkened graves with a frown. "Imagine opening each one in turn, and I'll be able to see the future that would provide."

Rae turned around in a slow rotation, doing as he asked. She'd almost made it all the way around when he suddenly stopped her.

"There—that's the one."

They hurried over through the fog and came to a stop in front of the large tomb.

"Jacob Riesler," Devon read aloud. "Anyone have any idea who that is?"

Luke shook his head. "None. But look at the dates. This guy had to be one of the first people buried in this cemetery."

Rae opened her hand and a crowbar appeared inside. "And I hate to disturb his slumber, but..." She wedged the handle in a crack in the stone and pulled with all her might.

The tomb sprung open with a mighty breath, like an old man gasping for air. A cloud of dust blanketed the four of them still standing there, all except Julian, who had the foresight to step aside.

"Thanks for the heads up, man," Devon huffed, coughing out a spray of dirt.

Julian grinned. "Don't mention it."

If there was one thing that turned out to be even creepier than breaking into a cemetery at night, it was slowly descending the stairs into the depths of a tomb. The flashlights did little to assuage their fears. Each time they whipped them nervously at a wall or down the darkened hallway, they half expected some undead zombie beast to be staring back at them. It wasn't until they'd already walked a good ten minutes underground that Rae realized there were torches lining the walls.

"Wait a minute," she whispered.

The group paused as she lifted her hand like she was blowing a kiss. The next second, a wave of fire lit the nearest one, which lit the next one, which lit the one after that. In no time at all, the dusty little hall was filled with golden torchlight, illuminating a strange-looking room just ahead.

"What is this place?" Luke asked quietly as they ducked inside, staring around in wonder.

"It's him," Rae answered grimly. "This is Cromfield's lair."

Luke shivered. "Like a bloody vampire."

It was worse than Rae could have ever imagined. There were images lining the walls. Pictures of people at all stages of life, all with a hand-drawn representation of their tatù pinned to the side. There were maps and charts. Strings attached to pins that stretched out all over the world, landing in a dozen different cities in a dozen different countries. Worse still were the files that lay strewn about a worktable set up in the center, documents from both the Privy Council and the Xavier Knights. Reports on all their current agents, all their current missions. Rae stifled a shudder as she saw Devon's face staring up at her from the heap. Perhaps the creepiest thing yet, was the half-drunk bottle of Coke sitting on a chair in the corner.

He had been here. Just recently. This was not some devastating place from the past, it was still in active use today.

"Rae..." Julian's voice trailed off as he gestured to a stack of papers, looking grim.

"What is it?" she asked as she came to investigate.

He just shook his head. "I think I'm going to be sick."

Rae glanced down in concern, and the next moment, she covered her mouth in a silent gasp.

They were experiments. The written record of over a hundred experiments performed throughout history. And judging from Cromfield's notes—they were experiments gone wrong.

"What are those for?" Molly asked, clearly shaken as she wandered over. "Who are they?"

Rae's voice was hoarse. It was like she was speaking from the darkest depths of her. "They're hybrids." She let the top file slip from her hand. "People like me."

Hybrids were supposedly an abomination? Cromfield certainly didn't seem to think so. In fact, from the looks of things, there was nothing he wanted more...

He'd kidnapped people, captured, brainwashed—who knows. All Rae knew for certain was that he was cross-breeding them, like they were animals. Trying to get the perfect hybrid child. From what Rae could see from his notes, not one of the children survived. In fact, most times, the mother died before she could even deliver—the child inside her was just too powerful. But that didn't stop him from trying.

He must have thought himself quite the scientist. He experimented on people with all sorts of tatùs—looking for the perfect combination for the ultimate power child. That he'd single-handedly murdered hundreds of people didn't seem to matter to him. Quite the contrary, the longer the hunt stretched on, the more he seemed to rise to the challenge. His notes became eerily hopeful, obsessively entrenched. He was firmly committed. Though why he wanted to create a virtual army of hybrids, Rae had no idea.

"What the hell is this?" Luke asked, snatching a piece of paper from the wall.

Rae took it from him without a word, holding it up against the map for context.

It was a list. A list of names with their corresponding coordinates listed on the map.

"What is that?" Luke asked again, staring at Rae with the utmost pity in his eyes.

"They're more hybrids." She hardly recognized the sound of her own voice. "They're the next ones he's after. He's going to bring them here too. Experiment on them. Breed them. Use that lunatic serum we read about in my mom's files. Who knows?" She couldn't stop her hands from shaking. "Either way, they won't survive."

"Then we have to get to them first," Molly exclaimed. "We have to warn them of what's coming. Take them somewhere safe."

"We will, Molls, we will," Julian assured her. He glanced automatically at Rae. "You have some kind of plan, right? You know what we're supposed to do next?"

She shrugged helplessly as the weight of his expectations and the responsibility of being the 'one that got away' fell heavy on her shoulders. What would Cromfield do to have her in his sights right now? He'd surely heard of her, with all the information he'd gathered on the PC. He'd gone through the trouble of brainwashing her mother, for heaven's sake. She was probably in a file down here with the rest.

A deep kind of rage Rae had never known simmered deep in her blood. The faces of each of his 'failed experiments' was burned into her brain, flashing before her eyes one by one.

He would pay for these crimes. Blood for blood. He wouldn't get away with this.

"Rae," Devon's voice called from the next room over. "You need to take a look at this."

She followed the sound of his voice, then stopped dead in her tracks as a piece of paper hit her in the face. "What the..." Her voice trailed off and she thought she might faint dead away.

It was her. A thousand times over.

Hand-drawn pictures of Rae hung from every inch of the room. Fluttering in the breeze made from the open door. Her jaw fell open as she took a step inside. Her own eyes stared back at her from every direction. Judging, wishing, asking questions she didn't have the answers to.

A feeling of muted horror settled in the base of her skull and she sank to her knees with a soft gasp. Devon was with her the next second, holding on to her tight as the rest of their friends filed into the room. Strangely enough, it was Julian that gasped aloud, ripping one of the pictures from the wall.

"This is...these are just like mine," he said in shock. "All those pictures I was drawing of you last year. I actually thought they were of your mother—you two look so much alike. But, no—it was you. They looked exactly like this." He stared around the room in astonishment. "Are we channeling or something...?"

Devon tuned him out and kept his eyes fixed on Rae. "It's going to be okay. We're going to stop this."

"How?" Her voice was faint. "How are we going to fix this?"

His eyes flashed. With desperation? Determination? She couldn't tell. "I don't know yet, but we're going to find a way. I'm not going to let anything happen to you. I swear it!"

"Rae," Molly knelt down beside her, holding out a folded sheet of parchment, "this was nailed to the door."

With trembling fingers, Rae smoothed out the paper. As she glanced down at the bottom, a half-choked gasp caught in her throat. "It's from him. Cromfield. It's addressed to me."

"What does it say?" Luke urged.

In a voice that was scarcely stronger than a whisper, she began to read:

My dearest Rae,

If you're reading this, then you've already far exceeded my every expectation. I've travelled the world searching for the likes of you, but in all my hundreds of years, I've found none that can compare. You are truly extraordinary. I hope you realize this.

By now you will have come to discover that it was I who took from you both of your parents. I hope, in time, you will understand my reasons for doing this. You see, Rae, they had served their purpose. They created you. Any further intrusion from them would only serve to separate us, and that is something I cannot allow.

This is because we are meant to be together, my sweet. In a world overrun with a sea of worthless mortals, it is you and I who will prevail. Who will go on to lead our people into the next great age. An age where people with abilities no longer need to hide in the shadows, but can rise to power and rule this earth as they were intended to.

I know this may seem like a radical thought to you at your young age, but I know that when given time, you will come round to my way of thinking. Be it one year, ten years, a hundred, even five hundred—you and I will be together and ascend to our rightful place in history.

That's all for now, my dear, but please know that there's a special place in my heart just for you. I can't wait for the day when I finally get to see you in person and make all these things known.

Be seeing you soon, my love,
J. Cromfield

A chilling silence followed her words—one that seemed to echo into the night. Devon hadn't released her the entire time she'd been reading, and when she glanced down now, she saw his knuckles were white with tension. Although a part of her wanted to automatically comfort him, a greater part of her was spinning out of control, further and further into the abyss. "What does that even mean," he murmured, his words sharp as a blade. "Even if it takes five hundred years? What's he talking about?"

"Isn't it obvious? I'm just like him, just like Cromfield."

Rae pulled herself to her feet, staring back at a thousand of her faces staring back at her. A burning feeling in the pit of her stomach was growing heavier and heavier, pulling on her body like it was dragging her straight down into the pits of hell.

She wanted to die, right then and there. "I'm freakin' immortal!"

~The End ~
Hidden Darkness
Coming January 2016

W.J. May

Sneak Peek of New Covers Book 7 & 8

Note from Author

I hope you enjoyed END IN SIGHT. If you have a moment to post a review to let others know about the story, I'd greatly appreciate it!

I love hearing from my fans so feel free to send me a message on Facebook or by email so we can chat!

I am working on a Christmas Novella release on Simon and Beth. A bit of a prequel so stay tuned for details!

I am also working on Hidden Darkness and have high hopes to continue the series after. I'm in no way ready to give up Rae's story. I feel like we are just starting to scratch the surface!

All the best, W.J. May

Newsletter: http://eepurl.com/97aYf

Website: http://www.wanitamay.yolasite.com

Facebook: https://www.facebook.com/pages/Author-WJ-May-FAN-PAGE/141170442608149

A Novella Prequel

of the Chronicles of Kerrigan
A prequel on how Simon Kerrigan met Beth!!

Check out W.J. May's Facebook Page or subscribe to her Newsletter for more details!!

The Chronicles of Kerrigan

Book I - *Rae of Hope* **is FREE!**
Book Trailer: http://www.youtube.com/watch?v=gILAwXxx8MU
Book II - *Dark Nebula* **is Now Available**
Book Trailer: http://www.youtube.com/watch?v=Ca24STi_bFM
Book III - *House of Cards* **is Now Available**
Book IV - *Royal Tea* **- Now Available**
Book V - *Under Fire* **– Now Available**
Book VI - *End in Sight* **– Now Availabe**
Book VII – *Hidden Darkness* **-**
Coming January 2016
Book VIII – *Twisted Together* **–**
Coming 2016

More books by W.J. May

Book Blurb:

Like most teenagers, Rouge is trying to figure out who she is and what she wants to be. With little knowledge about her past, she has questions but has never tried to find the answers. Everything changes when she befriends a strangely intoxicating family. Siblings Grace and Michael, appear to have secrets which seem connected to Rouge. Her hunch is confirmed when a horrible incident occurs at an outdoor party. Rouge may be the only one who can find the answer.

An ancient journal, a Sioghra necklace and a special mark force life-altering decisions for a girl who grew up unprepared to fight for her life or others.

All secrets have a cost and Rouge's determination to find the truth can only lead to trouble...or something even more sinister.

RADIUM HALOS - THE SENSELESS SERIES
Book 1 is FREE:

<u>Book Blurb:</u>

Everyone needs to be a hero at one point in their life.

The small town of Elliot Lake will never be the same again.

Caught in a sudden thunderstorm, Zoe, a high school senior from Elliot Lake, and five of her friends take shelter in an abandoned uranium mine. Over the next few days, Zoe's hearing sharpens drastically, beyond what any normal human being can detect. She tells her friends, only to learn that four others have an increased sense as well. Only Kieran, the new boy from Scotland, isn't affected.

Fashioning themselves into superheroes, the group tries to stop the strange occurrences happening in their little town. Muggings, break-ins, disappearances, and murder begin to hit too close to home. It leads the team to think someone knows about their secret - someone who wants them all dead.

An incredulous group of heroes. A traitor in the midst. Some dreams are written in blood.

Shadow of Doubt
Part 1 is FREE!
Book Trailer:
http://www.youtube.com/watch?v=LZK09Fe7kgA

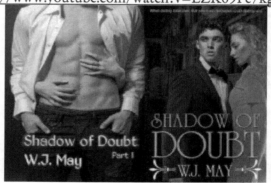

<u>Book Blurb:</u>

What happens when you fall for the one you are forbidden to love?

Erebus is a bit of a lost soul. He's a guy so he should be out to have fun but unlike the rest of his kind, he is solemn and withdrawn. That is, until he meets Aurora, a law student at Cornell University. His entire world is shaken. Feelings he's never had and urges he's never understood take over. These strange longings drive him to question everything about himself

When a jealous ex stalks back into his life, he must decide if he is willing to risk everything to be with Aurora. His desire for her could destroy her, or worse, erase his own existence forever.

Courage Runs Red
The Blood Red Series
Book 1 is FREE

Book Blurb:

What if courage was your only option?

When Kallie lands a college interview with the city's new hot-shot police officer, she has no idea everything in her life is about to change. The detective is young, handsome and seems to have an unnatural ability to stop the increasing local crime rate. Detective Liam's particular interest in Kallie sends her heart and head stumbling over each other.

When a raging blood feud between vampires spills into her home, Kallie gets caught in the middle. Torn between love and family loyalty she must find the courage to fight what she fears the most and possibly risk everything, even if it means dying for those she loves.

Free Books:

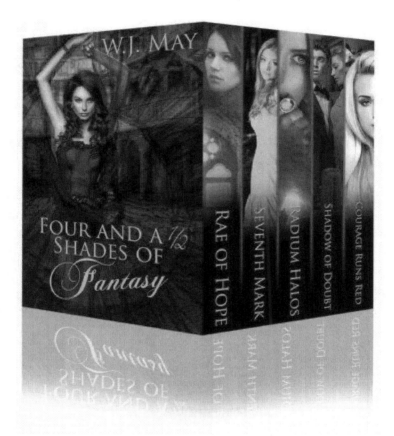

Four and a Half Shades of Fantasy

TUDOR COMPARISON:

Aumbry House——A recess to hold sacred vessels, often found in castle chapels.

Aumbry House was considered very special to hold the female students - their sacred vessels (especially Rae Kerrigan).

Joist House——A timber stretched from wall-to-wall to support floorboards.

Joist House was considered a building of support where the male students could support and help each other.

Oratory——A private chapel in a house.

Private education room in the school where the students were able to practice their gifting and improve their skills. Also used as a banquet - dance hall when needed.

Oriel——A projecting window in a wall; originally a form of porch, often of wood. The original bay windows of the Tudor period. Guilder College majority of windows were oriel.

Rae often felt her life was being watching through one of these windows. Hence the constant reference to them.

Refectory——A communal dining hall. Same termed used in Tudor times.

Scriptorium——A Medieval writing room in which scrolls were also housed.

Used for English classes and still store some of the older books from the Tudor reign (regarding tatùs).

Privy Council——Secret council and "arm of the government" similar to the CIA, etc... In Tudor times, the Privy Council was King Henry's board of advisors and helped run the country.

Don't miss out!

Click the button below and you can sign up to receive emails whenever W.J. May publishes a new book. There's no charge and no obligation.

Did you love *End in Sight*? Then you should read *Victoria* by W.J. May!

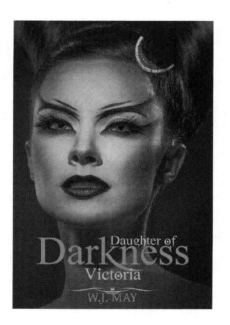

Victoria

Only Death Could Stop Her Now

The Daughters of Darkness is a series of female heroines who may or may not know each other, but all have the same father, Vlad Montour.

Victoria is a Hunter Vampire, one of the last of her kind. She's the best of the best.

When she finds out one of her marks is actually her sister she lets her go, only to end up on the wrong side of the council.

Forced to prove herself she hunts her next mark, a werewolf. Injured and hungry, she is forced to do what she must to survive.

Her actions upset the ancient council and she finds herself now being the one thing she has always despised -- the Hunted.

This is Tori's story by W.J. May. This is a novella. As a courtesy, the author wishes to inform you this novella does end with a cliffhanger. The next book coming out in early Autumn (or sooner) will continue the story.

This is an adult book series and does contain scenes for readers that are 16+

4 authors will each take a different daughter born from the Prince of Darkness, Vlad Montour. (Also known as Vlad the Impaler, an evil villain from history)

Blair – Chrissy Peebles

Jezebel – Kristen Middleton

Victoria – W.J. May

Lotus – C.J. Pinard

Also by W.J. May

Blood Red Series
Courage Runs Red
The Night Watch

Daughters of Darkness: Victoria's Journey
Huntress
Coveted (A Vampire & Paranormal Romance)
Victoria

Hidden Secrets Saga
Seventh Mark - Part 1
Seventh Mark - Part 2
Marked By Destiny
Compelled
Fate's Intervention

The Chronicles of Kerrigan
Rae of Hope
Dark Nebula
House of Cards
Royal Tea
Under Fire
End in Sight

The Hidden Secrets Saga
Seventh Mark (part 1 & 2)

The Senseless Series
Radium Halos
Radium Halos - Part 2

Nonsense

Standalone
Shadow of Doubt (Part 1 & 2)
Five Shades of Fantasy
Glow - A Young Adult Fantasy Sampler
Shadow of Doubt - Part 1
Shadow of Doubt - Part 2
Four and a Half Shades of Fantasy
Full Moon
Dream Fighter
What Creeps in the Night
Forest of the Forbidden
HuNted
Arcane Forest: A Fantasy Anthology
Ancient Blood of the Vampire and Werewolf

30221847R00127

Made in the USA
Middletown, DE
19 March 2016